Groover's Heart

Also by Carole Crowe

Sharp Horns on the Moon
Waiting for Dolphins

Groover's Heart

Carole Crowe

Boyds Mills Press

Text copyright © 2001 by Carole Crowe

Published by Caroline House
Boyds Mills Press, Inc.
A Highlights Company
815 Church Street
Honesdale, Pennsylvania 18431
Printed in the United Sates of America

U.S. Cataloging-in-Publication Data
   (Library of Congress Standards)
Crowe, Carole.
   Groover's heart / by Carole Crowe.—1st ed.
[156]p. :   cm.
Summary: When eleven-year-old Charlotte locates her long-lost uncle,
she discovers the truth about her parents' death and forges a new life
for herself.
ISBN 1-56397-953-5
1. Parents — Fiction. 2. Death — Fiction. 3. Life — Fiction.
I. Title.
813.54   21   [F]   2001   AC   CIP
00-103736

First edition, 2001
The text of this book is set in 13-point Minion.
Visit our Web site at www.boydsmillspress.com

10 9 8 7 6 5 4 3 2

For Zak and Alana,
and Morgan and Mollie—
And for their Grandpa Jack,
who has a heart filled with love

PROLOGUE

My name is Charlotte Dearborn, and I died when I was two.

To hear Aunt Viola, you would have thought I died just to annoy her. My parents, too, drowning when the ferry sank. Aunt Viola was my mother's older sister, and to hear her tell it, "When a silly romantic"—that was my mom—"runs off and marries a shiftless fool"—that was my dad—"sinking ferries is what comes of it."

So there I was, washed up on the beach like a little fish that missed the outgoing tide. Oh, did I mention? I'm not a ghost or anything. A doctor brought me back to life. You'd think I had a guardian angel, the way that doctor just happened to get a flat tire right where I needed him to be. Poor Aunt Viola. I know she doesn't believe in guardian angels, not after having a messy girl dumped in her neat home, a girl she never wanted. To hear Aunt Viola, growing up in her home saved me from a fate worse than death. (That was staying so messy and ill-mannered you would have thought I was raised in a barn.)

Not that Aunt Viola's beautiful house ever felt like my home, a place all warm and huggy. And believe me, I tried to feel happy and grateful. But the thing I felt most was the cold bite of clear plastic on the backs of my legs. Imagine covering perfectly good furniture with plastic! Why, you could squirm until the static electricity walked the hairs off your head and still never sink into those cushions. I guess Aunt Viola figured I'd slobber my food all over her custom-made furniture if she didn't keep it hothoused. But the truth is, I never chewed so much as a raisin outside of the kitchen—at least not when my aunt was home—just as Uncle Ed knew better than to light up his cigar in the house or in the car.

Don't get me wrong; things weren't all bad. Aunt Viola wasn't *cruel* or anything, not like Cinderella's stepmother. She was just, well . . . Aunt Viola. And one good thing about plastic-covered furniture: It makes a great farty sound if you plop down on it just right. Uncle Ed wasn't much of a talker, but he sure got a lot of mileage out of plastic. I don't know if he did it by accident or to cheer me up. Or maybe he needed cheering up himself. Aunt Viola's face would turn shrimp-pink, and Uncle Ed would act innocent. Like *what* farty sound? Sometimes we'd both plop down at the same time, and the air would burst from the plastic like from the woodwind section of my school orchestra.

But I didn't do it on purpose too often. Right from the start I knew better than to make a nuisance of myself. God might notice I wasn't dead after all and snag me in a hammer claw like a bent and rusty nail. God and Aunt Viola: Sometimes it was hard to tell them apart.

It might surprise you to know that for all of my eleven years—which includes the two from my pre-drowning life—I never once wished I lived with anyone else. But that's because I'd thought Aunt Viola and Uncle Ed were my only living relatives. Had I known there was a loving home just waiting for me, I would have sprouted wings when I drowned and flown there like an angel.

Once I thought I found that home. And I thought there wasn't a hammer claw in the world powerful enough to pry me loose. But that same hand of fate that took away my parents and left me behind feeling unwanted and unloved, well, it's reached right out of the sky again to steal my happiness for good. But I'm getting way ahead of myself. Let me start from the beginning—the day that led me to Groover.

ONE

Ours was the only Christmas tree at the curb, waiting for a trash pickup. With Christmas only one day old, I guess even rich folks wanted to hang on to the good feeling a while longer. From my perch on the roof, that poor tree looked so pitiful it could make a person cry. Not me, of course; it would take a lot more than a tree to make me cry. Maybe a broken leg or something, like my classmate got while skiing at Aspen. Still, just once it would have been nice if our tree didn't have to be all alone so close to Christmas.

Every year it was the same thing: Aunt Viola just had to go to Europe or some other faraway place with Uncle Ed, which left me for three whole weeks with Mrs. Riley. I think my aunt really wanted to bring me with them. It was that third week that caused all the trouble. By then my vacation was over, and I had to go back to school. Don't get me wrong. I had no complaints, not even about Mrs. Riley's snoring. Honest, I was glad she was coming the following day. After all, by taking care of me she earned enough money to visit her grandchildren who live far away. In fact, sometimes I'd pretend she was my grandmother, just to know what it felt like to be loved so much.

I watched silver tinsel blow across the lawn and snag in the evergreens. That cheered me up right away. This was the first year we'd had tinsel on the tree. (Tinsel and "tasteless" went hand in hand to Aunt Viola. And don't even *mention* stringing popcorn for decoration.) I rounded my mouth, trying to form halos with my breath like Uncle Ed used to make with cigar smoke before Aunt Viola decided he should quit. I huffed and huffed, but the wind snatched my halos away.

A tinsel tumbleweed bounced across the street and landed at Mrs. Rendlethorp's feet. She was our only nearby neighbor. (Rich people seemed to like land a lot more than they liked each other.) That chubby, bug-eyed dog of hers almost had a heart attack. You would have thought the tinsel was a Doberman, the way the dog yip, yip, yipped. If Aunt Viola wasn't so against dog hairs in the house, I would have gotten a big dog, one that wasn't afraid of a thing. I have to admit, though, it could make a person's eyes a little wet the way Mrs.

Rendlethorp managed to scoop that shivering pooch into her arms. Struggling home with it, she stared hard and mean at our poor Christmas tree.

Good thing Aunt Viola was still at the store. She could stand just about anything, except someone looking down on us. There'd be no tinsel next year if she spied it blowing all over creation.

I couldn't help but grin. We had tinsel this year, yes sir. All that private-school education that Aunt Viola insisted on just might be paying off. I swear, sometimes I was so smart I surprised myself. Soon as I saw that picture of a tinseled tree in one of those magazines about the rich and famous, I just knew it was the answer. Shrewd as can be, I left the magazine in the bathroom where Aunt Viola couldn't miss it. And sure enough, when it came time to trim the tree, along with those boring Victorian bows and the porcelain ornaments that were so expensive I wasn't even allowed to help decorate, Aunt Viola pulled out one box of tinsel.

Now if it was me, I would have bought a hundred boxes and tossed the tinsel in the air, letting it heap on the branches like silver snow. But it was fun, too, watching my aunt drape each individual strand until the tree looked perfect, like in the magazine. I hope one of the rich and famous gets a mind to string popcorn next year—and without those classy cranberries, thank you very much.

I tapped my feet on the shingles, thinking about life's possibilities. I sure wouldn't mind strings of colored lights instead of those boring little white ones. And maybe a brightly lit Santa Claus on the lawn, and Rudolph with a winking red nose. Just thinking about Rudolph the night he led Santa's sleigh made me burst into song right there on the roof. I didn't stop singing until my eyes came back to the lonely-looking tree at the curb. I folded my arms across my knees and rested my chin on them. I squeezed my eyes shut to clear my mind of all its ungrateful thoughts—and almost didn't hear our new Cadillac Seville pulling into the driveway.

I scooted closer to the chimney, doing a quick tinsel search of the lawn. One stray piece was tumbling toward the driveway. I held my breath until it caught on the rough bark of a maple tree. *Hang on*, I thought.

When I spotted Uncle Ed, I clamped my glove over my mouth to hide the cold laughter puffing out. It looked like a furry animal was sleeping on his head. As he climbed from the car, his new mink hat slipped sideways. He snatched it off, chomping on his dead cigar. For a second I thought he might do a pitcher's windup and fire the hat up onto the roof.

I don't know what made Aunt Viola think Uncle Ed would like a mink hat for Christmas. "Looks like roadkill," he'd muttered. Of course, *he* didn't say this within Aunt Viola's hearing—or he would have been roadkill, for sure.

I'd wanted to buy him a parakeet for Christmas because he'd had one when he was a boy. Aunt Viola said that was ridiculous; birds carry disease and poop everywhere and get squished underfoot when they land on the carpet. She didn't think much of a birdhouse in the backyard either. (The backyard was where Aunt Viola made Uncle Ed smoke his cigars no matter how cold it got.) "He doesn't need company in the yard, making a spectacle of himself like the Birdman of Alcatraz," she said. "He needs to quit smoking those filthy, stinking things is what he needs." For the third year in a row, she'd chosen a shirt for me to give him, a good one with pinstripes from a top men's store.

Uncle Ed and I were experts at pretending we'd gotten just what we wanted for Christmas. He loved his shirt, and I loved my cashmere sweater, new dresses, and soft leather gloves instead of the basketball and hoop that I'd asked for and dreamed about every night for months. I guess my aunt was right, though. Basketball was a dumb idea, just like owning a bicycle. There are so many hills in the neighborhood, my basketball might have bounced clear down to the wrong side of town. I've never seen the wrong side of town, of course, but I knew from Aunt Viola that living there is a fate worse than death.

I've never told this to a soul because I don't want my parents to look bad, but I have a feeling I once lived in a poor neighborhood with them. What else could explain this yearning that comes over me for all the things my aunt says are tasteless? And there's a framed photograph of me on our grand piano, taken before my parents died. The smile on my face looks like it could light up a forest of Christmas trees. The way I figure it, if I was that happy, then I must have been living someplace filled with tinsel and popcorn strands, colored lights and red-nosed reindeers. A place where a little girl could pedal her bike without flying downhill so far, so fast, she might never be heard from again. I guess this sounds awfully ungrateful, considering all the good fortune that's come my way, but I sure wish there'd been two more doctors with flat tires the day I died.

Aunt Viola gave the hat in Uncle Ed's hand a piercing look. He reached up to cover his bald head. That's when the Rendlethorps backed out of their garage. There was Uncle Ed, the hat poised in the air, watching my aunt watch their car, her eyes as round as silver dollars. It wasn't bad enough that Mr. Rendlethorp was wearing the same hat as Uncle Ed's—which explained my aunt's inspiration—but he was driving a brand-new car, and not a Cadillac either. It was a fancy silver car, the kind rich and famous people drive, with a gleaming metal grill.

There was only one car my uncle liked. That was an old Volkswagen Bug that Aunt Viola made him hide in the garage under a tarp so the neighbors couldn't see it. Poor Uncle Ed. He sure hated buying new cars all the time, but I guess he hated dealing with Aunt Viola more. A farty noise on a plastic couch was one thing.

Keeping up with the neighbors—well, that was something else.

He jammed the roadkill hat on his head, grabbed the packages from the car, and stalked up the walk, grinding that dead cigar like a licorice stick.

Aunt Viola paid him no mind. She was too busy watching Mrs. Rendlethorp glare at her from the car window. Finally, Aunt Viola spotted the tinsel. One of her stylish pumps shot out and pressed down on a clump, then the other shoe pinned a tumbling strand. Her feet were at odd angles, like she'd been photographed doing a tap dance. She stood that way until the Rendlethorps rounded the corner. If it didn't make me so sad, I would have laughed. Then Aunt Viola eased onto one knee, quickly stuffed the tinsel in her pocket, and sprang to her feet. Worrying about the world's opinion sure didn't leave time for tap dancing. Or for having any fun at all. Even from the roof, I could see the band of red spreading across her cheeks as she hurried into the house.

I inched my bottom along the roof and climbed through my bedroom window. Quickly, I tossed my jacket in the closet. I looked in the mirror, spit on my fingers, and flattened the cowlick in my brown bangs. I huffed into my hands to warm my face just in case anybody kissed me. Then I smoothed the lace collar on my new blouse and raced down the stairs.

"Charlotte, a lady walks down the stairs. She does not charge down like she was born in a barn."

"Yes, Aunt Viola."

"Did Mrs. Riley call yet?"

I shook my head.

"That woman. She knows we're leaving tomorrow morning, and I still don't know what train she's getting in on."

Uncle Ed was about to flip the hat into the back of the hall closet when my aunt turned suddenly. Instead, he blew on it, picking off imaginary lint, then hung it neatly on the coat hook.

"Edward, must you keep that disgusting thing in your mouth all day? I can smell it a mile away. The house reeks! Is this your idea of quitting?"

Uncle Ed maneuvered the dead cigar to the other side of his mouth. I sniffed the air but smelled nothing. I think Uncle Ed really wanted to quit smoking. Maybe chomping on dead cigars was his last stand against my aunt.

She pressed her fingers to her forehead. "I'm getting a headache. I can feel it coming on. It's the exhaust fumes, Edward. That car—"

Uncle Ed sighed.

"I have so much packing to do, and now a headache."

Uncle Ed's eyes lifted to the top of the stairs where the matched set of luggage had been packed and crowding the hall for three days. I shrugged at him, hands wide, and a smile flickered through his eyes.

"When we return, Edward, I think you should look around for a new car."

"We have a new car," he tried.

"I'm not thinking of myself," she said. "Those fumes could . . . destroy Charlotte's brain cells."

I hung my tongue from the side of my mouth and clutched my throat like it was too late. Uncle Ed bit the cigar harder to hide a smile.

My aunt lifted her hand to her forehead, and tinsel dangled from her sleeve. She shook her arm, and the tinsel strands flew against her chest like silver worms.

"Wow, Aunt Viola," I said, grinning. "Looks like you and tinsel were made for each other."

She huffed in annoyance as a worm snaked toward her collar.

"Edward, hurry into the garage. We need the tarp you're using on that vile Volkswagen. Wrap the tree in it. This tinsel is all over creation."

"Let the wind take care of it," he muttered. She held out his Christmas roadkill, and he jammed it on his head, then took his overcoat from her outstretched hand. A strand of tinsel leaped from Aunt Viola's chest to Uncle Ed's. It was hard to keep the grin off my face. As he stuffed his arm in the sleeve, she let out a gasp, her face scarlet. From an inside pocket of his coat, she ripped out a clutch of letters. Uncle Ed cringed at the sight of the forgotten mail.

"I don't believe it," she cried, pausing between every

word. "I don't believe it. One thing I ask you to do." She slapped the letters on the telephone table. "There are thank-you notes in here, Edward. What will people think?"

Uncle Ed didn't care what people thought, but he knew enough to keep his mouth shut.

"Don't worry," I said. "I'll remind Mrs. Riley to mail them while you're gone."

Idly, I shuffled through the letters. The last one caught my attention. Unlike the outgoing mail, this letter had been sent to my aunt, but a big "X" crossed out her name and address. In bold letters, she'd scrawled "Return to Sender," followed by three exclamation points.

My uncle stood perfectly still, staring at the letter in my hand. He reached for it, then seemed to change his mind, letting his hand drop.

"Who's this?" I asked him, peering at the return address. He didn't answer.

I called to my aunt, who was halfway up the stairs. "Who is C. Wattley in Southbay, Long Island?" You would have thought I'd thrown a bucket of cold water at her, the way she spun around, sputtering. She bounded down the stairs like she'd forgotten all her breeding.

"Charles Wattley is your aunt's brother," my uncle said quickly.

Aunt Viola's face turned a fiery red. If looks could kill, Uncle Ed would have dropped dead on the Persian carpet. She snatched the letter from my hands.

"You have a brother, Aunt Viola? But that means he's my uncle. And he was my mother's brother, too. How come you never mentioned him?"

It was the first time I'd seen my aunt at a loss for words.

"Is he married?" I asked. "Do I have cousins?" A new thought made my heart leap. *Do I have a big loving family I never knew about?*

Uncle Ed tugged his gloves on, an act that suddenly required all his attention.

"How come you're sending your brother's letter back?" I asked, reaching for it. My aunt swung it behind her back, as though it might burn my hand.

Finally she found her voice. "He's no one's brother, believe you me!" Uncle Ed opened his mouth to speak, caught a look from my aunt, and snapped it shut. Aunt Viola looked like she could breathe fire. "You just forget about him, young lady. I don't want to hear his name mentioned again!" She crumpled the letter in her fist.

"What did he do that was so bad?" I asked.

Aunt Viola didn't answer. Whatever he'd done, it made her rigid with anger. She looked like she was holding a live wire. I thought her eyes might shoot sparks at me and Uncle Ed. We both leaned away from her glare.

Then she marched up the stairs, talking to herself, her back as straight as a general's. On the landing, she summed up her thoughts out loud. "He's got larceny in his heart, that one. Make no mistake about it." She gave her head an angry shake. "Just like his father."

"Larceny?" I whispered to Uncle Ed. "What does that mean?"

My aunt spun at the top of the stairs, trembling. "You're still standing there?" she bellowed. Uncle Ed and I both jumped a foot. "I asked you to wrap up that tree, Edward! How many times do I have to ask you to do one little thing? How many times? You want people thinking we're trashy neighbors? Well, do you?" Her voice was choked with emotion.

I thought there wasn't another thing that could surprise me that day. But you should have seen my uncle's face. He wasn't annoyed by Aunt Viola's sharp tone. If anything, his eyes seemed to soften. He removed the cigar from his mouth. Gently, he touched my shoulder, then went outside.

Upstairs, the bedroom door slammed.

Quickly, I grabbed a pencil from the hall table and scribbled Charles Wattley's address on a piece of paper so I wouldn't forget it. *Larceny*, I thought. I knew it was something bad but didn't know exactly what it meant. In the den, I found our red dictionary and riffled through the pages. Frightened, I twice ran my finger under the definition of larceny: "The unlawful taking of personal property with intent to deprive the rightful owner of it permanently."

I smoothed the piece of paper and stared at Charles Wattley's address. My aunt's words rustled in my mind like dead leaves underfoot: *He's got larceny in his heart, that one.* What had my uncle stolen? I wondered. And who had he stolen it from?

TWO

I RUSHED TO THE WINDOW to see if I'd have enough time to use the phone. Uncle Ed was still wrestling with the Christmas tree. Keeping my eyes on the upstairs door, I got the area code for Long Island, dialed information, and waited for Charles Wattley's number. There'd be no chance to talk to him until my aunt and uncle left for Europe, but I could at least get his number. But what if he sounds mean? My private-school brain shifted into high gear. I could pretend to be one of those annoying telemarketers who always call at dinnertime selling alarm systems. But right away, I realized that wasn't a good idea. Someone with larceny in his heart might dislike burglar alarms on general principles and hang up. Maybe I'd pretend I dialed a wrong number. If his voice sounded nice, I'd call back and tell him the truth: "Uncle Charles, this is your long-lost niece, Charlotte."

I felt like I was on the roof again, imagining life's possibilities. I might have a whole bunch of relatives who couldn't wait to meet me. Just as I couldn't wait to meet them.

The operator's voice broke into my thoughts. "I'm sorry. There's no listing for a Charles Wattley in Southbay."

"There has to be!" I said. But there wasn't.

I'd only just learned about my new uncle, and already I'd lost him. Charles Wattley. Uncle Charles. Just thinking about him made me smile. I wondered if his friends called him Chuck or Charlie. *Charlie*, I thought. The name seemed to tug at my heart like a tender memory. "Charlie," I whispered. The sound of it brought tears to my eyes. Why would that name make me cry? I wondered. Again I whispered it. A feeling washed over me like I'd just been hugged. I must have known him when I was a baby, before my parents died, I thought. Why else would I get such a warm feeling when I hear his name?

Uncle Ed burst through the front door, his face red from exertion and cold.

I pounced before he got his coat off. "Uncle Ed! I already know Charles Wattley, don't I?"

He shook his head, getting his arm stuck in the coat sleeve. "You never met each other, Charlotte." Alien silver worms were everywhere by the time he got the coat off.

"Are you sure? His name sounds very familiar."

"He was in the army when you were born," Uncle Ed said. "He didn't even get out until . . ." For an instant, his eyes flickered away from my face, then came back. "Until right before the ferry accident," he finished.

"Oh," I sighed, disappointed. "This is going to sound weird, Uncle Ed, but when I thought of his name, I got this funny feeling like . . . like he loved me."

Uncle Ed glanced up the stairs. "Well, maybe you can trust that feeling, Charlotte. But you never met him," he said. And I believed he was telling the truth.

My aunt rushed from the bedroom and hurried down the stairs. "Edward, why didn't you tell me you were finished? Put your coat back on." Uncle Ed sighed loudly. "Charlotte, if Mrs. Riley calls, write down the train she's arriving on. We'll be right back."

Her words sent an electric jolt through my body and left a shocking idea sizzling at the edge of my mind.

"—listening to me, Charlotte? Close your mouth before it catches flies. What are you daydreaming about?"

"Where are you going?" I asked, evasively.

"*This* is going in a mailbox," she announced, holding up the crumpled letter.

"I'll mail it!" I reached for the letter, but she closed her fist on it.

"Why don't we just throw it away?" I cried. I sure wanted a look at that letter.

"I'm sending it back, thank you very much, because I don't want him thinking I read his letters."

Letters? I thought. Plural? He must have written before.

I forgot to hide my disappointment, and Aunt Viola caught the look in my eyes. "Are you thinking about him?" she demanded.

"I was just thinking that it would be really nice if you had a brother, Aunt Viola. He could visit us. And I could have another uncle! Wouldn't that be great?"

The hard line of her mouth answered my question.

"He must be a really awful person for you to hate him so much," I said.

My comment seemed to fluster her, as though she didn't hate him at all. Then she stiffened her lip and lifted her chin. "You just forget about hate, Charlotte. A word like that isn't . . . nice. But you forget about him, too, you hear me. Things have to be the way they are."

"But *why*?" I asked. "What did he do that was so bad?"

Rather than answer, she turned her back on me. She yanked the door open to a blast of cold air. "Edward!" she cried. "Those cookies she likes, we forgot to buy them!" He was beside her immediately, holding open the door.

"We'll find some, Vi. Don't worry."

Watching the Seville pull away, I saw Mrs. Rendlethorp walking her dog again. It now wore a red knitted sweater and matching cap. She sure loves her dog. I slipped my hand in the pocket that held my uncle's address, imagining his big loving family.

The phone rang, sending a tingle of fear to my stomach.

Staring at the piece of paper, I let the phone ring three more times before I finally ran to answer it.

"Oh, hi, Mrs. Riley," I said, trying to keep the wobble from my voice.

Then the words spilled from my mouth as I'd known they would from the first ring. "There's a . . . a family emergency," I said. "We were just going to call you. Me and Aunt Viola and Uncle Ed, we have to leave right away, so you can't come and stay with me." Before I hung up, I added, "Mrs. Riley, my aunt wants you to have the money, anyway. You know, so you can visit your grandchildren. We'll send you the check tomorrow."

I raced up the stairs and dragged a chair to my aunt's closet. I slid an old suitcase from the top shelf and brought it to my room.

Tomorrow I'd go to Long Island and find out why the name Charlie felt like love.

• • •

Early the next morning, I got out of bed and crept

into my aunt's television room. I pressed my ear to the wall, listening to the sound of the shower. I still had a few minutes left. I eased open the closet door and waved to the gray torso—no arms, no legs, no head—that stood on a metal stand. Long ago my uncle had told me that the sewing form was Aunt Viola's exact size and used for making her clothes. (Of course, I didn't mention that the form looked like it had lost weight.) There was a Singer sewing machine with a foot pedal in the closet, too. But never had I seen my aunt use it.

The day after I found out she could sew, I'd raced into a fabric store with my allowance, while my aunt tried on clothes in a shop next door. I held my hands wide to show the salesclerk Aunt Viola's size. I poured through a catalog until I found the perfect dress pattern, one that had a matching pattern in a child's size. I wanted to buy some pink pearl buttons, too, but the salesclerk said the buttons had to match the material my aunt selected. I was sure my aunt would teach me to sew. Together, we'd make all our own clothes. Mother and daughter dresses, exactly alike, only for an aunt and her niece.

I couldn't wait to see my aunt's eyes light up. Afraid he'd spoil the surprise, I didn't even tell my uncle. You should have seen my aunt's face when she opened the present. *I* was the one who was surprised. She rushed from the room, her face drained of color, my uncle right behind her. Later that day, I found the pattern in the kitchen trash, ripped to pieces. I never did find out what I'd done wrong. Not that it matters anymore. I'm too grown up for mother and daughter dresses now.

I pressed my ear to the wall again. My aunt was out of the shower, and I rushed across the room to wait. She was leaving for Europe in a little while, and I hoped she wouldn't change her daily routine. I sighed in relief when I heard her enter the room and rewind the VCR so she could watch the programs she recorded in secret. She eased into a reclining chair, swung the footrest up, and settled comfortably. A moment later, low voices filled the room. Still in my flannel nightgown, I hugged my knees and peeked from the closet door. This was my favorite time of day—just me and Aunt Viola watching the soaps.

You can't believe the troubles some people have in their lives. It makes me truly ashamed for feeling ungrateful at times. Poor Melissa got amnesia after her plane crashed in a jungle. Then she accidentally moved to her hometown and—you won't believe this—she fell in love with Doctor Tom, her own *brother*. Of course he didn't recognize her because she'd had plastic surgery. As soon as they both realized, she entered a convent. But it beats me why she picked an order of nuns who can't talk for the rest of their lives. Not one word. After Melissa, Doctor Tom fell in love again, "on the rebound" I'd heard Aunt Viola mutter. But the new woman is mean and sneaky, "a real gold digger."

Can I tell you a secret? Sometimes I don't even

watch the television screen. It's Aunt Viola I watch. With me and Uncle Ed, she's as rigid as that sewing form. With the strangers in her soaps, though, I've heard her laugh and cry as though she loves them with all her heart. I know my aunt is a good person. But I sure wish there was a magic dress pattern that would make her wear her heart on the outside.

The way she carried on that morning before leaving for Europe, you would have thought I was planning a pfeffernuesse rampage. Don't do this, don't do that. For goodness sake, how much trouble could I get into in the hour before Mrs. Riley arrived? Of course, in this case, I had more than an hour, since Mrs. Riley wasn't coming. Still, it's a miracle I even got a hug in with all my aunt's fussing.

"I can't believe that woman had to take a later train. I'll call the second we get to the airport, Charlotte. If Mrs. Riley isn't here yet—"

"Don't worry, Aunt Viola. She promised she'd be here."

She turned to me suddenly. "I hope you're not thinking of . . . of that letter," she said as though she couldn't think of anything else.

Recognizing her mind-reading look, I answered quickly. "No, Aunt Viola, I wasn't thinking about it at all. Honest."

She cleared her throat. "Charlotte, I left extra cash in an envelope. If you want to visit any of your school friends, Mrs. Riley can take you in a cab. Or . . . well, you can invite them over here."

I was so shocked I could hardly keep my mouth from catching flies. Aunt Viola never wanted my classmates over, making a big mess, especially when she was away.

"Thanks, Aunt Viola. But I think maybe they're all going away for the holidays, too." Again she shocked me by looking disappointed. I wished I could tell her the truth, that I wouldn't be around anyway, even if I had friends who could visit. Lying can sure put a hollow feeling in the pit of your stomach.

"Hurry, or you'll miss your plane," I cried, swinging the door open.

The concerned look blinked out of her eyes, and the old Aunt Viola was back. "Edward, are you sure you put all the suitcases in the trunk? You'd forget your head if it wasn't attached. . . . "

"Everything's packed, Vi."

Uncle Ed walked behind her to the car. Without warning, he flipped his mink hat behind his back. I caught it in midair. Turning, he gave me a wink, and my giggling almost gave him away.

It was only after they left that I became aware of being all alone.

Avoiding the phone call I needed to make, I plopped up and down on the farty plastic, but even that didn't ease my mind. I straightened the silver frames on the grand piano. They were studio photographs of my aunt and uncle, the only kind she liked. My aunt thought the early photograph of me looked like a cheap special from a discount store. (I guess it was my big tasteless smile she didn't like.) But I thought the later photographs of me looked like someone had airbrushed the life right out of my face. There were no framed photographs of my parents. And none of my uncle, Charles Wattley.

I lifted the piano lid and gently depressed each key from one end to the other. I'd started taking lessons, but Aunt Viola would only allow classical music in her home. Chopin is okay, I guess, but his music sounds awfully boring. I must have a jazzy heart 'cause I like to *hear* the fun I'm having, and *feel* it, right down to my toes. I suppose that's why I hate ballet lessons, so quiet and proper. Roll up the carpet and give me tap shoes— that's my motto, thank you very much.

I plunked the keys a little louder. Then I pounded them till my fingers hurt. Pretending to play ragtime, I scuffed up the rug with my dancing feet. Even after I'd closed the piano, the sour notes hung in the quiet house.

I almost wished Mrs. Riley was coming after all.

Finally, I called the taxi company. When the dispatcher told me the price to Long Island, I swallowed hard and hung up. Quickly, I counted the cash my aunt had left. There was more than enough money to get there, but what if my uncle didn't want a messy girl barging in on him? I shook that horrible thought away. Of course he'd want me to visit! And if he was married, I bet he and my new aunt would beg me to stay, and my cousins would, too. *Wouldn't they?* But what if Charles Wattley was single and lived in a tiny room in a boarding house? What if he was too poor to have visitors?

I could feel the tickle in my nose that comes right before the tears. I paced back and forth, working out a new plan. I snapped my fingers and stopped short on the Persian carpet. Of course! If I couldn't stay with my uncle, I'd bring him back with me. And if he was poor, I'd pay for everything.

I flipped through the Yellow Pages and finally dialed a number. A recorded voice gave me the entire schedule, but not a single train went straight to my uncle's town. After more phone calls, I realized I'd first have to take a train to New York City, then take the Long Island Rail Road to Southbay. Just the thought of it made my stomach jittery, but what else could I do?

Only one more train was leaving that day. To catch it, I'd have to hurry. But there was still something important left to do. I smoothed out a piece of Aunt Viola's blue stationery, blotted the goop from the end of a ballpoint pen, and composed a letter to my uncle, Charles Wattley. After folding it neatly, I slipped the letter into a matching envelope, my heart pounding to the *bong, bong* of the antique grandfather's clock. I took a deep breath, called for the taxi to the train station, then raced up the stairs with my fingers crossed. *What if the taxi came before Aunt Viola called to check up on Mrs. Riley?*

I knew from watching my aunt that you only traveled in your best clothes. First I put on my new dress, then the cashmere sweater. Next I tugged on new pink tights. They were a little long and sagged at the knees. I pulled handfuls of extra material from the toes, folded them under my feet, and slipped on my fur-lined boots. Studying myself in the mirror, I thought my aunt would approve.

Downstairs, I left my suitcase by the door. I slipped Mrs. Riley's check in an envelope and licked a stamp. I placed it in my pocketbook with the cash and the letter, wondering if larceny could be genetic. I hoped my aunt and uncle would forgive me for taking the money.

I hoped they'd forgive me for everything.

I stared at the phone, urging it to ring. "Hurry, hurry," I repeated. Hearing a car, I raced to the window. It was only our neighbors. Seeing Mr. Rendlethorp reminded me of my uncle's mink hat. I ran and took it off the coat rack. First chance I got, I'd throw it away. In three weeks, I'd definitely need somebody on my side.

At the sound of a honk, I again flew to the front window. "Oh no," I cried, seeing the taxi in the driveway. Fingers crossed, I wished as hard as I could. The telephone rang. I rapped on the window until the driver saw me. Then I rushed to answer the phone.

"Oh hi, Aunt Viola! . . . What do you mean? I'm

always excited to hear your voice. Uh-huh, Mrs. Riley got here, but she can't come to the phone." In a whisper, I said, "She has the runs." (I thought the runs was a brilliant inspiration.) "Do you want to hang on? She's got the runs really bad, though, and may be a while. I hope you don't miss your plane. Okay. Have a nice time in Europe. Don't worry about a thing. . . . His hat? No, it's not here. He must have lost it."

There was a shiny wet handprint on the receiver when I hung up.

My fingers fumbled with the buttons on my gray wool coat. I smoothed down the velvet burgundy collar, put on the matching hat, and tied it under my chin. My new gloves fit perfectly, the gray leather soft, the fur lining toasty warm.

The honking taxi hurried me out the door with my suitcase. The driver seemed surprised to see me alone until I gave a cheery good-bye wave to the house. "My grandmother's meeting me at the train station," I said, slamming the door. Then I squeezed my eyes shut— and tried to forget about larceny.

THREE

THE MOMENT I ENTERED THE STATION, I knew I had a problem. Would the ticket clerk sell to a young girl by herself? I studied the other passengers, wondering if I could ask someone else to buy my ticket. I heard an infant crying and saw a woman trying to soothe it on her shoulder. Her older child was a toddler, and she grabbed him with a free hand when he tried to run off.

I'll tell the ticket clerk I'm with them, I thought. But what if the mother already bought their tickets? Would the clerk get suspicious? I felt the sweat trickle from under my hat. The overheated waiting room was making me hot and sick to my stomach. The butterflies in my stomach didn't help. A man sitting by himself was snoring, his chin resting on his chest. Every now and then, he snorted like a pig, his head snapping up. Should I tell the clerk I'm with him?

Another man staggered into the terminal—the derelict I'd seen by a Dumpster. He was slipping a bottle of whiskey into a paper bag. His soiled raincoat came to the top of his old shoes. Flopping into a chair, he tipped the paper bag to his mouth and took a long drink before giving me a toothless grin. I shivered, thinking of Aunt Viola's reaction. Instead of the knit cap he had on before, the man now wore the mink hat I'd tossed into the Dumpster.

I stepped to the counter, looked into the clerk's eyes, and put on my best smile. "I'd like a ticket to New York City, please. That's my grandfather," I said, pointing over my shoulder. From the back, the derelict looked like Uncle Ed, a well-dressed traveler. "See, what happened was, Grandpa already bought his ticket, but now I'm going with him and—" Before I could finish, the clerk punched out the ticket and asked for the money.

Boarding the train, I stayed close to the woman with the children. She didn't seem to mind at all when I sat beside her. And I didn't mind when her son climbed into my lap. On the long trip, I made believe the woman was my mother. Having a loving family sure felt good. How could my aunt reject her own brother? What awful thing had he done? When the boy fell asleep, he snuggled against me. First I made believe he was my brother. Then I pretended he was my cousin. If my new uncle was married, I might really have a cousin, just like the little boy in my arms.

● ● ●

I accidentally followed the wrong crowd when I got off the train at Penn Station. Instead of staying underground and following signs to the Long Island Rail Road, I ended up on an escalator that went to the street. I never saw so many people in one place in my whole life. Taxi horns blaring, folks dodging the cars across the street . . . why, it's a wonder anyone had time to return my smiles. And the fumes in New York City—I bet they kill a million brain cells a minute! Still, I thought my excitement would lift my feet off the pavement: They sell hot dogs on the street! Honest, sauerkraut and all. Aunt Viola says hot dogs are common and never cooks them. Common or not, they sure tasted good. No wonder so many people live in New York City, dying brain cells and all.

I heard a *clop, clop* and turned to see a mounted policeman on a big horse. I was the shortest person around, but his eyes still found me. Tapping his heels against the horse's belly, he moved closer.

I turned and waved at the crowd. "I'm over here, Grandma!" I felt like a city slicker when the policeman's horse clopped away. Grabbing my suitcase, I ran back to the escalator and rode it up and down twice.

Nervously, I strode past the Long Island Rail Road ticket clerks. Would they sell me a ticket? Would they call a police officer? No one paid any attention to me. But I didn't want to get caught when I'd come so far.

Beside me, a woman slid money into a vending machine. Leaning closer, I watched the machine spit out a ticket. The solution to my problem! I purchased a ticket to Southbay, then checked the schedule. I had time to spare before the train left. Not taking any chances, I located the right track for the Southbay line, so I'd know exactly where it was.

There are so many stores and restaurants in Penn Station, I bet a person could live underground forever. Wandering around, I bought a sweet blender drink called Orange Julius, the first I'd ever tasted. I approached a flower stall, wondering if my uncle liked flowers. I pictured him in a garden with my new aunt surrounded by tulips and daffodils and roses. I bet they can't wait for spring! I thought. I studied the flowers in pots of water and decided on a cheerful bouquet of bright pink daisies. The flowers had no scent, though, so I bought one yellow rose. I slid it into the middle of the daisies and sniffed the bouquet. It smelled as pretty as it looked.

I didn't have too much time left, but I had enough to find a restroom. A bag lady was sitting on the cold tile floor. A bad odor steamed from her body in the hot restroom. Her cart was filled with ragged clothes and empty cans and all kinds of junk that seemed useless to me. Her hair, gray and dry, stuck out like she'd gotten a fright. She wore two dresses, red long underwear, and a baggy woolen sweater.

You wouldn't have thought she could work in all those clothes. But there she was with a pair of scissors, trying to shorten a man's overcoat that looked like it came from a Dumpster. The scissors stopped moving.

Her eyes shifted toward me like black magnets.

Frightened, I backed against the wall and tried to edge around her.

Another woman entered the restroom but didn't see me. I wanted to tell her I was there, but I was afraid she might realize I was alone and tell the police. She walked right by the fanned-out coat as though the bag lady were invisible. I inched farther into a corner, waiting for the woman to finish. On her way out of the restroom, she clicked her tongue and huffed in annoyance, pressing her finger under her nose in disgust.

I started toward the stall but stopped. Did the bag lady know people clicked their tongues because she smelled bad and had no home? What if she did know and felt terrible about it?

Her red swollen knuckles looked painful, the dull scissors useless against the thick cloth. My knees felt weak and my heart thumped in my throat, but I tiptoed toward her.

"Hello," I whispered. "Do you need any help?"

The woman turned to stone.

I stuffed my gloves in my pockets and knelt beside her. I took shallow but quiet breaths, so she wouldn't think I noticed her smell. I placed the bouquet on the floor. Her eyes narrowed; she leaned away from me. Cautiously, I reached for the hem of the coat.

"Try it now," I said, holding the fabric taut. At first I thought she'd yank it from my hand, but she hesitated.

"Go ahead," I said gently. "I'll hold it tight, so it's easier to cut."

Slowly, she chopped about five inches off the coat.

"There," I said. "I bet it'll fit perfectly now."

Suddenly, her dirty yellow fingernails clamped on my wrist.

I tried to pull away, but they dug into my skin. She pulled me close, but her eyes didn't focus on mine. Instead, they seemed to look far beyond me. "Don't you cross that street again." She shook my wrist, her face urgent and frightened. "Don't you get run down, you hear me?" I nodded hard, wondering who she was seeing in her wet and cloudy eyes.

She looked around suspiciously, as though returning from a long-ago memory. Shoving my hand away, she stood, pulled the coat on, and scooped up my flowers, stuffing them in her cart. She hurried from the restroom, the coat's ragged hem trailing on the floor.

I grabbed my suitcase and rushed into a stall. I wondered if the bag lady had once lived in a nice house with her own daughter. I wondered if once she had smelled like bubble bath and someone was glad she was home. I didn't come out of the stall until I was sure I wouldn't cry. And I almost missed the train.

It was late afternoon when I arrived in Southbay. I sure had a lot of grandparents that day. The last one was meeting me at the station. The conductor waved good-bye when I pointed to a woman across the way. I don't think it was the cold that made me shiver when the train left me all alone on the platform. What if my new relatives didn't want me to stay? What if my uncle was single but refused to come back with me? What if he didn't like me one bit? No, that's not possible, I thought. I whispered his name, *Charlie,* and that same warm feeling came over me.

There were no cabs around, but I found a street map in the phone book and copied the directions. It didn't look far to the house, but I thought my toes would freeze off before I got there. At least there were no hills. And the lawns didn't grow all the way to the street either, like in my neighborhood. Instead, there were sidewalks. Sidewalks where kids could walk and ride bikes and play basketball. Rich people could sure use some cement mixers, I thought.

Turning a corner, I saw a large body of water. I realized I'd never been told where my parents had drowned. I breathed the salt air, watching the gulls float through space. A breeze was blowing, but the water looked as flat as a pie plate. Then a sea gull landed, skidding on the frozen surface like a clown. Does my uncle take his kids swimming here in the summer? I wondered. I could almost hear them laughing and splashing. Feeling happy, I hurried on.

At the end of the street, a boy who looked my age was tossing newspapers from his bicycle. I read the street sign. My uncle's house wasn't very far. The boy stood on the pedals and pumped toward me. *He could be my cousin.* We hadn't even met, and already I liked him. I watched him propel the bicycle over tree roots that had cracked the sidewalk wide open. I bet he rode better than a movie stuntman. I'd tell him that as soon as he reached me. I was smiling so hard I almost didn't duck in time when the newspaper whizzed over my head.

"You almost hit me!" I cried. He made a rude noise with his mouth and kept going, watching me over his shoulder. I hoped my uncle didn't live on the wrong side of town.

My heart fell when I finally reached his address. The house paint was peeling; the windows were bare of curtains. A loose shingle flapped on the roof. The front yard was filled with clutter—an old tire, a bent license plate, lots of weeds. I tugged the slip of paper from inside my glove, thinking I'd made a mistake. But the address matched the faded numbers on the house.

I pushed open the creaking gate, and it slipped from the rusty top hinge. Gingerly, I climbed the wooden steps to a wraparound porch, stepping over a broken board. No one answered my knock. I rang the bell. Still no answer. I peered through the windows on the porch, but they were too dirty to see through. The suitcase was much heavier as I walked away. If my uncle ever lived here, he's moved, I thought. None of the other houses on the block looked abandoned. Only the one I'd been counting on.

I stood on the sidewalk wondering what to do next. Skidding to a stop, the paperboy almost knocked me over with his bike.

"Be careful!" I yelled, dropping my suitcase and leaping out of the way.

We glared at each other in silence. His bike had no fenders, and the leather seat was cracked. A canvas newspaper bag hung from rusty handlebars. The boy had freckles and large blue eyes. He wasn't wearing a hat, and his red ears looked cold. I didn't let myself feel sorry for him.

"I'm certainly glad you're not my cousin!" I said.

"Your *cousin*? I wouldn't be your cousin if you paid me. What're you doing snooping around here?" he asked.

I lifted my chin. "I'm looking for Charles Wattley."

"Who's he?"

"I thought he lived here," I answered.

"I know who lives here, and it's not him."

Trying not to cry, I picked up my suitcase and walked away.

There was a junkyard next door. At least it looked like one. A broken sign I couldn't read hung sideways over a shop door. Tires and rusty parts were piled in front of the garage. Old cars were parked everywhere. The place looked as abandoned as my uncle's house. Behind me, I heard the boy's squeaky bicycle wheels.

I peered through the shop door. "Hello? Anybody here?" The garage owner just had to know where my uncle had gone. But what if I couldn't find my uncle? Soon it would be dark. Where would I spend the night? Remembering the homeless bag lady, I started to shiver—from the cold and from being so scared.

The paperboy was leaning on one leg, balancing his bike. His face was screwed up as he studied my clothes. "Why are you dressed like that?" he asked.

"Like what?" I said, looking down at myself.

"Like that!"

My pink tights had gotten very baggy. I turned my back on him and tugged them up. Otherwise I looked just like Aunt Viola would have wanted.

A grunt came from inside an old car with an open hood. Ignoring the boy, I walked toward the car. A man was lying across the front seat, working on wires under the dashboard. There was a hole in the bottom of his left shoe.

"Got a *girl* here looking for some Charles guy," the boy shouted. "Found her snooping around next door." When the mechanic sat up, the paperboy jerked his thumb in my direction.

The man's deep brown eyes widened when he saw

me. He held absolutely still, staring until my face reddened. Is everybody rude in Southbay? I wondered.

He glanced at my suitcase but didn't mention it. Walking toward me, he opened his mouth to speak. Instead, he frowned at the engine. He looked so upset I thought there were tears in his eyes.

"Need some help with the engine?" I asked.

He buried his head under the hood. When he finally answered, his voice sounded hoarse. "You could hold this down while I try to start it." He tapped a metal part to show me. Again I caught him staring at me. Abruptly, he looked away, banging his head on the hood, before hurrying to get back in the car.

I tugged my gloves off, pressed my finger on the part, and squeezed my eyes shut. "Okay!" I called.

"No way he's getting that junk heap running," the boy said.

The engine roared to life.

I gave the boy Aunt Viola's squinty-eyed glare. "He got it started pretty good if you ask me."

The man turned the engine off but sat in the car for so long I thought he'd forgotten me. It was getting dark, and I had no place to stay. My teeth chattered, and the cold air made the tears hurt my eyes.

When I picked up my suitcase, the man finally got out of the car.

He took a deep breath and let it out slowly. "Hello, Charlie," he said to me. "Joey, say hello to my niece."

FOUR

"You're Charles Wattley?" I cried.

"Folks call me Groover," he answered, softly.

Turning, I stared at his shabby house but remembered my manners and lowered my eyes. I even forgot to ask how he knew I was his niece. But I guess no other girl my age would be looking for him.

"My name is Charlotte," I said. "Why did you call me Charlie?"

"Yeah, how come she's got a boy's name?" Joey muttered. "It's as dumb as her clothes."

My uncle grabbed one of my gloves from the fender and wiped his greasy hands on it, then stuffed it in his back pocket. *Was it a mistake or a symptom of larceny?* I wondered. I snatched the other glove away.

There was a thin crescent scar by the side of his right

eye. When he smiled it disappeared in a crinkle. "Your parents wrote while I was in the army," he answered. "They always called you Charlie."

"They did?"

So that's why the name was familiar. *I'm Charlie,* I thought. My mother and father must have loved me so much I could still feel it in the sound of my name. Before I could stop myself, I burst into tears.

Joey pedaled away like I might be contagious.

Groover picked up my suitcase and walked me toward the house. I followed him through the broken gate and up the rickety stoop. At the door, I looked down the street, smiling through my tears. In the growing darkness, colorful lights twinkled on houses and bushes. On a rooftop, a glowing Santa Claus seemed to be climbing into the chimney. Across the street, a menorah for Hanukkah shone in the window, every candle lit. All of the houses were decorated with lights. All but Groover's. His house was dark.

He pushed open the door and waited for me. I stepped over the broken board, then stopped abruptly.

"You have lights, too, Groover," I said, gazing up at the dark strand above the door.

He looked up in surprise. "So I do," he said.

• • •

Groover didn't say a word while he read the letter.

Only once before had I forged someone's handwriting.

That was when my friend at school had forgotten a permission note for a class trip. She said the note I'd written for her looked exactly like her mother's handwriting. I hoped I hadn't lost my touch. Twice Groover peered at me over the top of the paper, then reached for the cookies I'd brought. Powdered sugar sifted like snow onto the bare floor. I leaned my elbow on the pile of clothes that shared the sofa with me. My stomach filled with butterflies, waiting for him to finish the letter.

Finally he folded it up. "I'm glad my other letters were returned accidentally, Charlie. I was afraid you might have moved."

I sighed in relief. "Nope, we're still living in the same house."

I knew writing a nice letter from Aunt Viola was the right thing to do. Groover would have felt terrible knowing how his sister really felt about him. It isn't right to hurt a person's feelings—even if he does have larceny in his heart.

"And I'm glad your aunt was happy to hear from me and wanted us to get acquainted while they're in Europe," he added. "It's about time we met."

"That's what I thought! Aunt Viola tried to call and ask you to come stay with me and Mrs. Riley, but you have no phone."

"So she said in the letter. How did you get here, Charlie?"

"How? Oh . . . well . . . I took a taxicab," I answered.

It was a lie but not a hundred-percent lie. I did take *one* cab, after all. "It seemed like fate when Mrs. Riley had a multiple heart attack right after they left. So, instead of mailing Aunt Viola's letter, I figured I'd come and invite you myself. You'll come stay with me, won't you? There's a nice guest room and everything."

"I'm afraid I can't do that, Charlie."

"Oh." I bit into another cookie, but the sweet taste was gone.

"I have the shop to run, such as it is. Folks are waiting to get their cars back."

"That's okay, Groover. I understand." I waited for an invitation, but none came. "I guess I better get going, huh? Aunt Viola says uninvited company is like bad fish. They both smell to high heaven."

Groover picked up my coat but folded his arms around it. I tugged, but he pressed it tightly against his heart.

"Charlie—" He lost his voice and looked down. Running a hand through his hair, he tried again. "Charlie, I know you're used to a lot better . . . but I sure do wish you'd stay with me while your aunt and uncle are in Europe."

"You do?" I looked around at the messy living room and patted the soft sofa. It was much too late for plastic covers. Powdered sugar was everywhere.

Like Groover, it was hard for me to speak—but that's because I was smiling so hard.

"Thanks, Groover," I said. "I bet Aunt Viola will be as happy as anything that we're finally getting acquainted."

He slipped the letter in his shirt pocket, looking away. "I'm sure she'll be thrilled," he answered. "I can't wait to see her face."

• • •

Waking up the next morning to a smiling face on the ceiling—even if it was a water stain—felt like a good omen. I smoothed the sheets, then remade the iron folding bed, hiding the small rip in the blanket. Groover had said he intended to clean the room, but I decided to do it myself. I wanted him to know I'd be a good houseguest.

There were faded curtains on the bedroom window. I wrote my name on the dusty sill. A tree grew all the way to the window, the bare branches thick and strong. They looked perfect for holding a tree house. Outside my bedroom window at home, there was nothing but green sod and empty hills. It gave me a good feeling, seeing a house right next door. Silky pink curtains framed the neighbor's window. I wondered if a girl my age lived there.

Groover was sniffing a milk carton at the refrigerator when I walked in the kitchen.

"Good morning, Groover."

His eyes crinkled with pleasure at the sight of me. I

would have hugged him. But I didn't want him to think he'd never get rid of me.

Still smiling, he stared at my clothes.

"Something wrong?" I asked.

"That's a . . . nice outfit," he said. He was wearing a plaid flannel shirt and faded jeans.

"Thank you. Aunt Viola has exquisite taste, don't you think? It was a Christmas present."

Clearing his throat, he studied the refrigerator again. There wasn't much in it—a jar of pickles, a bar of butter, and some furry-topped dishes that looked like my science experiments.

Groover tossed the milk carton in the trash. "How about I take you out to breakfast," he said. "Seems we finished all the cookies last night. I'll tackle your room when we get back."

"I already cleaned it," I said.

"You shouldn't have, Charlie. I told you I'd take care of it."

"I wanted to," I said. I studied the empty refrigerator. "Aunt Viola left me lots of money, Groover. I'll pay, okay?"

Groover blinked slowly. "It's okay, Charlie," he said, softly. "It's my treat."

Outside, our next-door neighbor waved from her car. Groover groaned as she hurried over.

"I'm running late," she said, smiling at me. "Only have a minute."

"What a shame," Groover mumbled. "Roberta, this is my niece, Charlie. She's here for a visit."

"Nice to meet you, Charlie. What a wonderful surprise! Where are you off to all dressed up?"

"We're going out to break—"

Groover coughed loudly.

"Breakfast!" Roberta said. "Come to the diner. That's where I'm heading right now."

"Okay!" I cried. "That's great!"

Groover sighed, and Roberta grinned at him. "Toodle-oo," she said, waving her fingers.

• • •

The seats in our booth were covered in red vinyl. I bounced, but they didn't make noise.

"So how you been, Groov?" Roberta asked, standing by our booth. She wore a black waitress uniform, a pencil poking from the red hair piled on her head.

"Getting by," he answered, as he studied the menu—although Roberta had already taken our order.

"You're looking good these days," she said. "Considering."

"Considering what?" I asked.

"Roberta, you think you could put our order in so Charlie and I don't die of starvation?" Groover's remark didn't faze her.

"Don't you be a stranger, Charlie. I love company."

"Okay. And you can visit us, too, right, Groover?"

Groover narrowed his eyes at her over the menu. Roberta snatched it from his hands, her green eyes twinkling. "Thank you, Charlie. Don't mind if I do."

I whispered when she left. "She sure is pretty, Groover."

He grunted.

"Do you have a girlfriend?" I asked.

"Just you, Charlie." From his eyes, you would have thought he meant it.

"Too bad you never wrote to *me*, Groover. Maybe my letters wouldn't have gotten lost in the mail like Aunt Viola's did. How many letters did you write?"

The coffee cup stopped on the way to his mouth. "Just a few," he mumbled, setting it down. He pushed quarters into a small jukebox on the table.

"Don't worry," I said. "Your letters will never get lost again. From now on, *I'll* check the mailbox at the end of our street, every single day."

He tried to smile, but a thought seemed to pass through his eyes, a thought that made him look away. We flipped the lists behind the jukebox glass. Groover liked the same songs as I.

"Wow," I said, as Roberta walked toward us. The whipped cream and strawberries were piled so high on my pancakes that they almost toppled over. I covered my lap with the paper napkin, trying hard to remember my manners. Groover must have been a mind reader. Twice during breakfast he signaled Roberta for more whipped cream. He hardly touched his own food, though, while I brought him up to date on my life. Instead he watched me and listened like he couldn't get enough.

"That was pretty clever, Charlie. Leaving the magazine in the bathroom for your aunt to see."

"Yup, you've got to be thinking every second to put one over on Aunt Viola." Draining my orange juice, I studied him through the glass. I licked the juice from my top lip and tasted whipped cream. "Groover, how come you don't have a phone?" I asked suddenly.

He scratched his head. "It got turned off a while back when I forgot to send in the payment on time. Guess I just got used to not having one."

"If you got one again, we could call each other. I'll give you our unlisted number. Hey, I know! Maybe you'll see a picture of the rich and famous with popcorn on the tree. You could call and tell me, and I'll get the magazine. We'll be in cahoots!"

Groover's eyes shone when he smiled. "Cahoots sounds good to me, Charlie."

Even as he spoke, I could sense my aunt's disapproval. Would she let me take his phone calls? Would she try to keep us apart? *Maybe I should tell Groover the truth.*

"Something wrong, Charlie? . . . Anything you want to talk about?"

"Nope! Not a thing," I blurted. How could I tell him

how Aunt Viola felt? How could I hurt his feelings?

"You're sure, Charlie?" His eyes were so intense, you would have thought he already knew my secret.

"As sure as anything," I answered, then quickly changed the subject. "So, Groover, how come you took your Christmas tree down already?"

At that moment, Roberta appeared with a coffee-pot. "Yeah, Groover, how come your tree is down so soon?" She sloshed hot coffee over his thumb.

"Ouch. Thanks, Roberta," he said, shaking his hand. "You must make great tips working here, you're so good."

A look of innocence replaced her grin. "You didn't answer Charlie," she said sweetly. "The Christmas tree?"

"My niece and I are having a private conversation, Roberta. You mind scalding somebody else?"

Grinning, Roberta flounced away.

I leaned in to whisper. "I think she likes you, Groover. I bet she'd make a good girlfriend."

He leaned close, too. "Not in a million years," he said.

I rested my chin in my palms. "So what about your tree?" I asked.

He threw his hands up. "There was no tree, Charlie. I didn't get around to it this year, that's all." He slid from the booth, throwing bills on the check. "Here she comes again with hot coffee," he grumbled. "Let's get out of here before she boils me alive."

Roberta winked at me as I hurried after him. "Toodle-oo," she called. "Don't be a stranger, Groover— if you know what I mean."

He rolled his eyes as he eased through the door.

In the parking lot, we waited for the car to heat up. Old junk heaps take longer to heat than new Cadillac Sevilles.

"Where's your other glove?" Groover asked.

"Mmmm . . . I guess I lost it."

"Try these," he said, pulling his own gloves off. They were already warm from his hands, and so big for me they looked like puppets. We backfired out of the lot.

At a traffic light, I danced my puppet hands in the air. Laughing at me, Groover missed the green light. The driver behind us held the horn until the light changed again. A rusty green car shot around us. The driver continued honking, I guess to make sure we knew he was mad. The woman in the front seat was staring straight ahead. In the backseat, a boy turned. It was Joey. He stuck his knuckle in his nose, pretending he was picking it right up to his brain. If he'd *had* a brain.

"Uck, your nasty paperboy," I said. "Are those his parents?"

Groover nodded.

"His father has a mean face," I said. "Just like Joey's."

"Joey's a good kid. Maybe you'll be friends."

"Not in a million years," I answered.

Two blocks from the house, we saw a man dragging a Christmas tree to the curb. I guess Aunt Viola's not the only one who likes to travel around the holidays. At the stop sign, Groover didn't pull away. Instead, he stared in the rearview mirror. Suddenly he shifted gears, threw his arm around the back of the seat, then drove backward to the end of the block. He jumped from the car, opened the trunk, and tossed the tree inside. Before I had time to worry about larceny, we were driving away, tinsel blowing all over creation.

Twice he turned to look at me on the way home. "Charlie, are all your clothes so . . . *nice?* Don't you have any play clothes?"

"Play clothes?"

He nodded. "That's what I figured."

Fifteen minutes later, we were shopping in a Wal-Mart. And I picked out a flannel shirt exactly like Groover's.

FIVE

"FOLLOW RIGHT BEHIND ME, CHARLIE. Watch where you kneel, or you'll fall through the ceiling. Stay on the boards, not the insulation." I felt like Alice in Wonderland, crawling after Groover in the dark attic to the middle section, where the peaked roof and flooring allowed us to stand.

"They're here somewhere," Groover said, pulling on a lightbulb string that hung from the ceiling.

Cobwebs trailed across my face like tinsel and snatched at my flannel shirt. I brushed dust from the knees of my new denim overalls. The flooring extended to the other side of the attic. Stacked boxes leaned dangerously. There was so much junk, I bet a bag lady could poke around forever. Or a girl my age. A Flexible Flyer sled was propped upright, and ice skates, both a black and a white pair, hung by the laces from nails.

Groover stopped what he was doing and stared at my cloudy reflection in a full-length mirror. Amazed, I stepped closer. It could have been a magic mirror, the girl in play clothes a complete stranger. I could almost feel my aunt's disapproval. I spit on my fingers and smoothed my cowlick. But I couldn't stop smiling at the new me.

Groover shook his head as though clearing it of something painful and resumed his search.

"Whose are these, Groover?" I lifted the white skates off the peg.

"The black skates are mine," he said in a quiet voice. "Those are your mother's."

A red pom-pom dangled from one lace, the other pom-pom missing. The blade felt cold under my fingers. White shoe polish powdered my fingertips when I rubbed the leather. It was the first time I'd held anything that belonged to my mother. An ache filled my chest. Bending over, I lined my foot against the skate. I sat on the floor, the skates in my lap, imagining my mother as a girl my age.

"There's a lake not far from here." Groover knelt beside me. "We skated every night during the winter and made bonfires to keep warm. Your mother liked to spin on the ice. She thought if she spun fast enough she'd lift off and fly to the moon." He reached for the skate but took his hand back without touching it. "One year we had a severe cold spell, and for the first time the bay froze solid. Your mom and I skated all the way across."

"Groover? . . ."

He waited.

Softly, I asked, "Did the ferry sink around here?"

Absentmindedly, he rubbed the scar near his eye. "No," he finally said. "You were living on the north fork of Long Island with your parents. This is the south shore. Your parents were . . ." He leaned close, as though wanting to tell me something important. But he let the moment pass.

"I've never gone skating, Groover. Can we skate across the bay together?"

He shook his head. "It hasn't been cold long enough. But the lake is safe. We'll go there before you leave."

Leave, I thought. It was easy to forget I would have to go away.

I removed my new high-top sneakers and tugged my mother's skate on, first the one with the faded pom-pom, then the other.

"If those don't fit, there's—" He stopped himself.

"There's what?" I asked.

"Nothing," he said quickly.

"I can wear fat socks," I said. "These will fit fine." I clicked the silver blades together. "Didn't Aunt Viola skate, too?" I asked.

Frowning, he shook his head. "Only when we were all little. When she got a little older . . ." He looked around, then slid a box from under a cobweb. Pushing it toward me, he said, ". . . she didn't have time for anything but this." His voice sounded tired. The white web clung to his brown hair and made him look old. He got up and continued searching for the Christmas ornaments.

I pulled the lid off. The box was filled with sewing patterns—for dresses, skirts, blouses, even coats. Instead of skating, Aunt Viola had made her own clothes. I wondered why she didn't sew anymore. And why she'd torn up the pattern I once gave her.

"Here they are," he said, shaking a box. Inside, broken glass tinkled. An image of Aunt Viola's expensive ornaments passed through my mind. When Groover tossed the box aside with a crash and picked up another, I covered my mouth to stifle a giggle.

That night I decorated a Christmas tree for the first time. I had no idea it could be so much fun. I bet Aunt Viola didn't know it could be fun either. That's the trouble with making a Christmas tree look perfect. Groover stood on a stepladder, reaching up to place the angel on the top of the tree. If Aunt Viola had seen our tree swaying, if she'd been there holding her breath— why, just thinking about her made an ornament slip from my hands. Groover jumped from the ladder and crunched the ornament underfoot. Don't ask me why we both thought that was the funniest thing in the world.

With our arms folded, Groover and I eyed the tree. Our angel was missing a wing. I smiled, thinking this was a good omen—a guardian angel with one wing could never fly away.

"Sorry the stores were out of tinsel, Charlie. Looks a little bare, doesn't it?" The tinsel from the previous owner was wrinkled, much of it missing.

"It's the most beautiful tree I've ever seen, Groover." I looked up at him. "Maybe we'll have tinsel next year."

For a moment, his eyes held mine, then he looked away. I guess he figured I was fishing for an invitation to visit. But already I was hoping for so much more.

I felt an ache in my chest that matched the look in Groover's eyes. "I know what it needs," I cried, trying to recapture our good mood. I raced into the kitchen and searched the cupboards.

"What are you looking for?" he called from the living room.

"We can string some popcorn for the tree!"

I had opened the last cupboard when Groover came up behind me.

Quickly, he pushed the door closed. "Sorry, Charlie. The popcorn cupboard is bare."

He was right about that. The only thing inside was a bottle of whiskey.

"Maybe Roberta has some popcorn!"

"Charlie—" But I raced from the house before he could stop me.

A few minutes later, Roberta returned with me, carrying a bag of goodies. Instead of greeting Groover, she gave the popcorn jar a shake and marched through the living room. She yelled from the kitchen: "What happened to your maid? She have a nervous breakdown?"

Groover growled at me as he walked toward the kitchen. He tried to look mad that I'd invited her over. But one thing about Groover: There was no hiding the twinkle in his eyes when he felt good. Just like there was no hiding the sadness that came into them later.

Once the corn was popped, we carried heaping bowls into the living room. Roberta took needles and thread from her pocketbook. Giving Groover a look, she flung clothing and his blanket and pillow from the sofa to make room for the three of us. Groover never slept in his bedroom. You'd think he was a visitor in his own home, someone who didn't really belong there—or anywhere—like me. In the fireplace the logs crackled. Together, we strung the popcorn until we had so many strands Groover said Orville Redenbacher would need a wheelbarrow to haul his money to the bank. You should have seen the popcorn on our Christmas tree. Honestly, the rich and famous don't know what they're missing.

After that, we made peanut butter sandwiches for dinner. Groover stopped Roberta mid-sandwich, removing the knife from her hand. Patiently he said,

"Roberta, first you *butter* the bread, *then* you put on the peanut butter." He looked like an orchestra leader demonstrating with the knife. Behind his back, Roberta waved her hand, silently mimicking his words. "Keep it up, Roberta," he said, like he knew exactly what she was doing without seeing her. Leaving the kitchen with a stack of sandwiches, he kept a straight face. "Yours is on top, " he told her. The fingers of his leather glove waved from between two slices of bread like a toodle-oo.

Roberta followed him out of the kitchen, carrying two bottles of ginger ale, while I cracked open an ice tray for my Dr. Pepper.

Then I remembered the bottle of whiskey.

Aunt Viola and Uncle Ed sometimes chilled wine when company came. Should whiskey be chilled, too? I wondered. I took the bottle from the cabinet and put it in the refrigerator, just in case.

On the sofa between Roberta and Groover, I felt like we were a family. I remembered the train ride with the mother and children. But this feeling was so special it was hard to swallow my sandwich. And even harder to hold back the tears.

After dinner, I helped Roberta make hot chocolate topped with Marshmallow Fluff. We carried the cups to an old upright piano in the living room. There were no silver-framed photographs on top. No photographs at all. Unlike my aunt's shiny grand piano, I couldn't see my face reflected in the worn wood.

Roberta made a big display of sweeping the clutter off the piano top with her arm. "Oops. Hope that old orange peel wasn't an heirloom, Groov," she said.

There was one thing she didn't sweep from the piano though. A bronze sculpture of a little girl in a swing that hung from a tree branch. The girl was laughing, her eyes so lifelike it wouldn't have surprised me if she blinked. I ran my fingers over the statue, enjoying the cool feel of it, like the blades on my mother's skates.

Groover lifted the piano lid, and we shared the bench, Roberta watching over the rim of her raised cup. Some of the keys were slightly depressed, all of them yellowed. I played a few bars of Chopin until Groover took my finger and played "Jingle Bells" with it while I sang along. Then his fingers ran up and down the keys, and I bet we sang every Christmas carol ever written.

"Boy, Groover, I never knew playing the piano could be so much fun. Too bad I didn't move in with *you* after my parents drowned!"

I heard Roberta draw in a breath. Groover lifted his fingers from the keys, and Roberta almost touched his hand, as though to make him continue. But she stopped herself, stuffing her hands in her sweater pockets instead.

Before I could think of something to say, something that would put the smile back on his face, Groover closed the cover over the piano keys and left the room. I was sure my remark about living with him had ruined the evening. What else could it be? Groover was a lot more fun than Aunt Viola, but I figured even he didn't want the trouble of raising a pesky girl. Silently, Roberta and I collected the dirty cups and brought them to the kitchen.

We found Groover staring into the refrigerator, looking surprised. He tried to close the door, but Roberta stopped it. She reached in and slowly withdrew the bottle of whiskey. She spoke through her teeth, her eyes flashing with anger. "Why don't you just send Charlie packing right now?"

"Get off my back, Roberta."

"It's been six years," she said. "What's wrong with you? Now of all times?"

I didn't know what they were talking about. I only knew I'd made a mistake moving the bottle. But why should whiskey be hidden in a cupboard?

"It's the holiday season, Roberta. Do you mind? I bought it right before Christmas . . . in case friends dropped by." He snatched the bottle from her hand and slammed it on the counter.

"What friends? You're in trouble, Groover. You've crossed over a line. You keep heading in this direction, you might never get back. Give the Judge a call."

"Can I ask you something, Roberta?" His voice sounded genuinely puzzled. "How is it that with all the . . . the *corn* popping you do, you still have time to run my life?"

They stared at each other hard, as though forgetting I was there.

Roberta looked at the worn linoleum on the floor, the window without curtains, then back at him. "I don't know what gets into me, Groover," she said. "Obviously your life is so manageable these days, you don't need help from anyone."

Cold air blew into the kitchen when she slammed the refrigerator door. I could feel it all the way to my heart.

SIX

In the middle of the night, I bolted awake, but couldn't recall the dream that had frightened me. I tried to get back to sleep, but tossed until I was rolled in my sheet like a mummy. It was thoughts of the whiskey bottle that kept me awake. I crept down the stairs, trying not to wake Groover. In the kitchen, I stood at the cupboard. My heart aflutter, I finally looked inside. The whiskey bottle was back on the shelf. Unopened. What did Roberta mean about six years? Why did she tell Groover to call a judge? What kind of trouble was he in? I tiptoed back to the living room. Groover was asleep on the sofa. I wished I could make him feel comfortable living in his own home—comfortable living with me. I sat on the floor beside him. At that moment, I already loved him with all my heart. Listening to his soft snores, watching his sweet face, I felt like I was sharing a special moment with him, like watching the soaps with Aunt Viola. I promised myself I'd never ask to live with him again. I'd never do anything to hurt him.

• • •

The next day I realized I'd made a terrible mistake: I'd forgotten all about the letter Aunt Viola had returned to Groover.

From the front door, I watched him take the envelopes from the mailman. Was he holding the returned letter?

Grabbing my jacket, I ran outside just as a Cadillac pulled up, an Eldorado, not a Seville. Something changed in Groover's eyes when he saw the car, and he slipped the mail into his back pocket. The man who got out of the car had thick white hair, but his eyebrows were black and bushy. He wore a camel-colored overcoat and a white woolen scarf around his neck and looked as nice as Uncle Ed.

I heard Groover release a long breath as the man approached him.

"Hi, Harry. Good to see you," he said.

"It's been a while, Groover." They shook hands.

"Yeah, well, you know how it is. I've been kind of tied up. This is my niece, Charlie."

"How do you do, Charlie," Harry said, shaking my hand, too. "I heard you were here. Was this a surprise visit, Groover?"

Harry and I both waited for Groover to answer.

The quiet made me jittery, and I put on my best smile. "Aunt Viola wanted Groover and I to get to know each other while she and Uncle Ed are in Europe," I said. "She feels terrible that we haven't met before, and she can't wait for Groover to visit her in Connecticut."

Harry's bushy eyebrows lifted in surprise, then lowered into a frown as he studied Groover and me. I was glad *he* hadn't read my forged letter. He stepped closer to Groover. In a low voice, he said, "I heard you were expecting some friends to stop by for a drink around the holidays." Groover shot an angry look at Roberta's house. And I wondered why he would care that she'd mentioned the whiskey bottle to Harry.

"Charlie and I are doing fine, Harry," he said.

"Glad to hear it, Groover. And I'm glad to hear your sister can't wait to see you again." The men stared at each other.

Finally, Harry looked around. "You're the best mechanic I know, Groover. Why don't you get that sign back up with your name on it? You deserve this business."

"I know that, Harry," Groover said, looking down.

Shaking his head, Harry said, "I was in the neighborhood. Just thought I'd stop by."

"I appreciate it, Harry. Thanks. It's good to see you."

"If you want to see more of me, you know where to find me."

When Harry got in the car, Groover moved forward as though to stop him. But he stepped back and watched Harry drive away. He continued staring long after the street was empty.

As we walked toward the house, I remembered the mail. I hung back, trying to peek at the letters sticking from Groover's back pocket. He turned as though he realized what I was doing. He put his arm around my shoulder and pushed the mail deeper into his back pocket.

All day I tried to read his face. I found him watching me as well.

During dinner, I nervously nibbled the edges of my hot dog bun. "Groover, did you . . . get any interesting mail lately?"

The fork stopped at his mouth. I might have imagined the tenderness in his eyes. "I never read the mail, Charlie. It's nothing but junk mail, anyway. I always throw it out without looking at it."

"Oh," I sighed, happily. "That sounds like a great idea." Then I bit into my hot dog and finished my beans.

After dinner, Groover disappeared into the attic. Smiling, he came down with the ice skates. He hung my mother's pair over my shoulder. It's a good thing he did, too. I felt so light and happy I might have floated up to the ceiling and bumped my head.

The moon was full and glowing the night I skated for the first time. At the lake, Groover put on his own skates, then knelt in front of me and laced up my mother's. Like a magician, he pulled a blue pom-pom from his pocket to replace the red one that was missing. When he stood, he looked like a friendly giant. He reached down for my hand and pulled me upright. My feet scooted out from under me, and I fell with a plop, dragging Groover with me. His laugh must have carried to the far side of the lake. We tried again, and this time I didn't fall. But my ankles folded in like a cardboard box, and I clopped along while Groover glided beside me. At first we skated close to shore to avoid the throngs of people. My ankles got tired, but I wouldn't give up.

And then I was balanced perfectly on the blades. Groover let go of my hand, and I pushed off with my toe. He skated backward at my side. When I teetered, he reached out and steadied me.

"Look!" I cried. A goldfish the size of a trout was swimming under the ice. We skated across the lake with the fish following us everywhere. I almost said, "Let's get a goldfish for home!" But I bit down on the words, locking them inside.

A long line of kids skated toward us holding hands. Joey was at the end, huffing like a frozen dragon. He yelled something, but the only word I could make out was *whip*. He grabbed my hand when he got close, and though I tried to shake free, he wouldn't let go. He raced beside me as I clumped along, trying hard to keep up.

"Here we go!" he shouted. Then the most incredible thing happened. The front of the line stopped and whipped the rest of the line around—rocketing Joey and me away like Olympic speed skaters. I was screaming to the sound of Joey's laughter, then my own laughter filled the air. The wind frosted my face, and I thought we'd never slow down.

Suddenly, Joey dug his blades in, stopping himself instantly. Flying ice chips sparkled in the moonlight. We were nearing the end of the lake.

I looked ahead, and saw a tree speeding toward me.

"Stop!" Joey shouted. But I didn't know how to stop.

I waited to smash into the tree with my eyes squeezed shut. Then an arm wrapped around me. It was Groover guiding me away from the danger. We slid to a stop in front of Joey.

My knees were shaking. I didn't know whether to thank Joey or be angry at him.

"Want to do another whip?" he asked.

My ankles collapsed.

Again Groover came to my rescue. "We're leaving soon," he said. "Maybe next time."

Joey skated backward to watch me. I gave him a small wave. He waved back, then turned, racing away

Before we left, Groover showed me how to spin.

Hugging his arms to build speed, he looked like a whirling genie. When he stopped, his eyes were shining. I remembered what he'd said about my mother, how she'd wanted to spin fast enough to fly to the moon. I dug the jagged tip of my skate into the ice: I didn't want to spin. I didn't want to go to the moon. The only place I wanted to be was right there with Groover—forever and ever.

We warmed ourselves by a fire blazing in a steel drum. I could see myself reflected in Groover's glowing eyes. Behind us, I heard a voice shout in anger. It was Joey's father yelling at him, not even caring that people were watching. Joey flinched as he squeezed past his father to get in their car. Maybe he knew what was coming. His father's hand shot out and slapped Joey hard on the back of the head.

Groover's gloved hands turned into fists. Fire flashed in his eyes as he moved toward Joey's father.

I don't know what might have happened if Joey's mother hadn't jumped from the car. We watched his parents glare at each other over the hood before they got back in the car with Joey and drove off.

Walking to the car, Groover kept his arm tightly around my shoulder. He left the heater on high until I stopped shaking.

"Let's go for a drive," he said.

I sat close to him as we cruised around the neighborhood, looking at Christmas lights. It was the night before New Year's Eve, and I knew they'd be taken down soon. Groover pointed out Joey's house, the green car parked in the driveway.

"Too bad Joey can't get his father to do a whip near the end of the lake," I said. "Splat! That'd be the end of him."

Groover just cleared his throat. "How about some ice cream?" he said.

We stopped at a 7-Eleven and bought a gallon of mint chocolate ripple and one of cherry vanilla because we couldn't make up our minds.

The frozen bay was silver in the moonlight. A car sped past us and veered from the main road, bumping over frozen ruts toward the bay.

"It's Joey's father!" I cried, recognizing the car.

It drove onto the ice and away from shore. Groover blasted his horn, shouting from the window. "Hey, George! Stop!" But the car kept going, fishtailing across the ice.

"He can't drive across the bay," Groover said. "We'd need another month of this cold before the ice could hold a car." Groover parked, flashing his headlights and honking the horn repeatedly.

On the ice, the car lurched to a stop. It got lopsided as the right tires broke through the ice. Groover leaped from our car and sprinted toward the bay.

"Groover, come back!" I cried, racing after him.

He pulled his jacket off, and I grabbed for his arm when he stepped on the ice. "Don't go, Groover, please."

He stared down at me, then back at Joey's father. "I have to help him, Charlie!"

"But he's mean! *Please* don't go," I sobbed. "You might drown . . . like my parents."

We heard a loud crack. The car bobbed as though floating.

"Oh, Charlie," he whispered, hugging me. "I'm so sorry." Quickly, he let me go, walked as far as he safely could, then crawled on his belly.

He slipped into the circle of water around the car. I could see him in the moonlight, struggling with the door.

The car sank lower and lower and finally disappeared.

Then Groover was gone, too.

There was nothing on the ice, nothing for as far as I could see. Over and over, I cried his name. Just when I thought he was gone forever, his head bobbed to the surface. He dragged himself onto the ice, then pulled Joey's father out after him.

Headlights appeared. Car doors slammed. People rushed toward the sound of my screams.

Groover inched toward shore on his belly. People rushed forward with blankets. Finally Groover stood on land and helped Joey's father up. The man looked shorter than I remembered. Then I saw his face in the moonlight. It was Joey, not his father, Joey who had stolen the car. His teeth were chattering, his lips blue. But when I waved, he poked his hand through the blanket and bent his frozen fingers at me.

A brown car lurched to a stop and Joey's mother jumped out of the driver's side. When her husband got out and tried to join her, she pushed him aside and ran to her son, sobbing.

Groover walked toward me. He looked like an ice sculpture, his hair and eyebrows frozen. But not his eyes—they were as warm as ever.

"Ch . . . Charlie," he stuttered. "You mind if we skip the ice cream tonight?"

I hugged him so tightly I thought he might melt into a puddle.

The next day, the local paper wrote about the "hero" who saved a drowning boy. But I knew what a real hero Groover was. Lots of people might risk their lives to save a child. But how many would do it to save a man as mean as Joey's father? I'm sure glad Groover didn't listen to me that night. It could almost make a person believe in guardian angels.

SEVEN

THE NEXT MORNING, I could hardly take my eyes off Groover.

"You sure you don't want more hot tea?" I asked.

"I think I'm pretty well thawed out by now," he answered.

He'd been staring into the open cupboard. I eased the door closed on the whiskey bottle and stepped in front of it.

"You have plans for tonight, Groover?"

"I sure do, Charlie. I'm going to watch the ball drop with my best girl. Unless you have some other plans?"

"Nope. I'm all yours."

For as long as I could remember, I'd spent New Year's Eve alone. Unless you counted Mrs. Riley, who was always snoring long before midnight. I made

Groover take me to the store so we could shop for our party. We bought three bags of pfeffernuesse cookies, the last in the store, and some pretzels and chips and candy. For dinner we brought pizza home, hot and gooey. It was the first time I'd ever eaten it. Groover showed me how to flip the end of the slice up so the cheese would stop sliding onto my shirt. No wonder Aunt Viola hated pizza.

After dinner, I stuffed the box into the trash can outside. I stood in the cold and stared at Roberta's house, but her car wasn't there. Did she have a date? I wondered. Or was she working? I slipped back in the house for a pencil and paper. I peered over my shoulder to check on Groover, then sprinted across the yard.

Later I dumped onion soup mix into sour cream, the only dip I knew how to make. I put chips and pretzels out just like Aunt Viola does, although she's never used paper plates.

Near midnight, we turned on the television to watch the ball drop in Times Square in Manhattan. Groover looked surprised when the doorbell rang. Quickly I stuffed his sheet and blanket under the sofa cushions, brushed potato chip crumbs from the coffee table and sat down. I crossed my feet at the ankles and folded my hands on my lap like I'd been taught.

Groover opened the door, then turned and narrowed his eyes at me.

"Hi, Roberta," I said. "What a nice surprise."

We counted down the remaining seconds of the year. When the ball reached the bottom, there was a moment of awkwardness. I waited for them to kiss each other like you're supposed to do at the stroke of midnight. Groover scratched his head, then stuffed his hands in his pockets. Roberta examined her nails.

"Anybody can kiss *me* if they want to," I finally said. Red-faced, Roberta and Groover started laughing.

We banged pots out the front door. If we'd had a phone, I would have called Joey and wished him a Happy New Year. Groover sat at the piano, the first time he'd played since the night we trimmed the tree. His fingers flew along the keyboard, and he pounded out the happiest music in the world. You should have seen his eyes when Roberta held up a kazoo. I wondered how long she'd been carrying it with her waiting for just that moment. She tooted away while Groover boogie-woogied on the piano.

Then I started to dance as though my feet had a life all their own. Tinsel blew from the tree and crinkled the room with silver. I kicked and twirled and slapped my feet on the hardwood floor, and Groover could hardly sing for his laughter.

It was the best New Year's Eve I'd ever had. If only I hadn't ruined it.

"Groover, you know what I was thinking?" I was breathless from dancing, and maybe from the joy of not losing him the night before. "I should live with you all the time. Wouldn't that be great?" The smile slipped off Groover's face like he'd been wearing a mask. I pressed my hands over my mouth, wanting to take back the words.

Roberta turned to him, a tender look in her eyes. I heard her whisper, "Need any help with this, Groov?"

I don't think he even heard her. He leaned toward me, like there was something he had to tell me, something so important you'd think his life depended on it. Then his eyes emptied and he looked away, fingering the scar near his eye.

I wanted to cry out: *I didn't mean it about living with you! I was only kidding!* But I couldn't speak any more than Groover could. He lowered the lid on the piano keys.

"It's getting a little late," he said, trying to smile, trying to pretend nothing was wrong. But everything felt wrong at that moment. And I wondered if it was *too* late—too late for Groover and me.

• • •

I came awake, frightened. In the darkness, I felt danger all around me. Branches tapped at my window like frozen fingers. The floor was icy underfoot as I left the warm bed and crept toward the stairs. I shivered, but it wasn't from the cold. At the top of the stairs, I listened for Groover's soft snoring. I wanted him to be asleep. I wanted him to be safe. I heard footsteps below, and the creak of the sofa.

I forced myself down one step. Then another. Finally, I saw Groover and my legs turned to rubber. I sat and stared through the wooden spindles of the stairway, as though watching someone who was behind prison bars.

The unopened bottle of whiskey sat on the coffee table in front of Groover. His hands were clasped in his lap, his knuckles white. His face looked pale in the dim glow of a lamp. The look in his eyes took my breath away. I'd seen Aunt Viola and Uncle Ed drinking wine with their guests. But never in all my life had I seen anyone stare at alcohol the way Groover was staring at that bottle. *Why did he look so afraid?*

He sat back, his face disappearing in shadow.

Did Groover want to drink? Or was he trying to stop himself from drinking? And what difference did it make, either way? My fingers hurt from gripping the spindles. *Why was Groover afraid?* I didn't know what might happen if he drank. But from the look in his eyes, I knew nothing would ever be the same again if he opened that bottle. Not for him. Not for me. And never for the two of us together.

He leaned forward suddenly. His ghost-white face came out of the shadow. I yelped in fright. My foot slipped, and I bounced down a step. Groover sprang from the sofa.

"Charlie, what are you doing up so late?"

"I couldn't sleep, Groover. I had a bad dream.

Is everything okay?" I knew my voice sounded as shaky as his.

He stared at the whiskey, pulling back as if it were poison. He shook his head as though clearing it. "Sure, Charlie. I couldn't sleep either. . . . I think I was having a nightmare myself."

The terrible look was gone from his eyes. But what if it came back? What if he opened the bottle?

I started down the stairs, but he crossed the living room. "It's late, Charlie. What do you say we both try for some sleep?" He leaned over and kissed my forehead. Before he could pull away, I hugged him tightly.

At the top of the stairs I waited. I didn't go back to bed until I heard Groover go into the kitchen and the cabinet door open, then close.

In bed, I kept seeing his face. I knew that my remark about living with Groover had upset him. I wasn't mad at him, though, for not wanting to live with me. You can't force people to love you, no matter how much you love them. Hadn't I learned that from living with Aunt Viola? I was mad at myself for ruining everything. I was mad at myself for upsetting him. I knew what I had to do in the morning for Groover's sake.

I rolled over and cried myself to sleep.

• • •

While Groover was in the shower, I crept downstairs and quickly removed the ornaments and lights from the Christmas tree. Dead pine needles rained through the branches onto the floor. The bare tree brought a lump to my throat. Popcorn strands were heaped in the corner like dirty snow.

On top the angel was barely hanging on.

As I was dragging the tree out to the curb, Joey almost beaned me with a newspaper.

"Sorry. I didn't see you," he said, leaning on his bike. "What are you doing out so early?"

"I thought I'd take the tree down before I leave," I answered.

"Leave? You mean for the store or something?"

"No, I might be going . . . home." I'm sure the disappointment on his face matched my own. "I'm glad you didn't drown," I said. "Was your father mad about his car?"

He shrugged like it didn't matter, but his cold ears got redder.

"Maybe Groover will give him a good deal on a junk heap."

We stood there, grinning.

"Well, I better go in," I said, turning.

"Wait a minute," he called.

My jacket wasn't buttoned, and I started shivering.

Joey didn't seem to know why he'd stopped me. "How come you're not wearing the weird clothes you came in?" he asked.

"They weren't weird!"

"Were so."

Again I turned and again he stopped me. "Wait! . . . uh, you owe me twelve dollars." He stuck his hand out. "Pay up!"

"I do not!"

"Do so. You're living with Groover. So you owe me twelve dollars for delivering the paper . . . and don't forget my tip."

I shifted my eyes to the newspaper in the bushes. "You don't *deliver* the newspaper. You throw it all over creation." I spun around and stomped off.

"Red sneakers are dumb!" he shouted.

Roberta was retrieving her newspaper from the lawn. Grinning, she shook her head. "Joey, you keep picking on that girl, she'll think you have a crush on her."

Joey pedaled away, his face flaming.

Roberta started walking over, but I hurried into the house. I wanted to tell her about the whiskey bottle and the terrible look in Groover's eyes. I wanted her to know that he might be in trouble like she'd said. And if he was in trouble, so was I. But I figured Groover had enough on his mind without having Roberta mad at him again.

I was sweeping the floor when he walked into the living room with his hair still wet from the shower. The crescent scar near his eye was so white it might have glowed in the dark like the moon.

He took the broom from my hands. "Why did you get rid of the tree?" he asked.

"That old tree was a fire hazard, Groover. Hope you don't mind. I just figured you'd be safer without it."

He studied me closely. "Safer? Something wrong, Charlie?" he asked, softly.

"Nope, nothing's wrong," I answered. "If you have a vacuum, Groover, I'll clean up the rest. . . . " He wasn't listening. He was staring toward the front door. His foot kicked the fallen angel as he crossed to my suitcase.

"You going somewhere, Charlie?" he asked.

I took a deep breath and threw my hands out. "Gosh, Groover, if I stay here any longer, I'll be just like bad fish. And you must have an awful lot of garage work to catch up on."

I reached for the suitcase, but he moved it back, gripping the handle so tightly, his knuckles turned as white as they'd been the night before.

"It's okay, Groover. I'll just take the same trains back that I took—" I clamped my mouth shut, remembering I'd lied about my trip to Southbay.

The color drained from his face. "Trains? Charlie, are you telling me you were alone in the city? You didn't take a cab all the way from Connecticut?"

"It was no problem, Groover. People were really nice to me."

I'd never seen him so upset. Except when he'd looked at that bottle. "Charlie, promise me you'll never do something like that again."

"I promise," I said, reaching for my suitcase.

Again he moved it to the side. "Charlie, is there a reason you want to leave?" I could tell from the confusion on his face that he didn't know I'd seen him stare at the whiskey bottle.

I wished I could shout: *I don't want to leave. Not ever.*

"Honest to goodness," I said, "that Mrs. Riley is lost without me during the holidays. I bet she's already over her heart attack and wishing she could come stay with me. I'll call her, so you don't have to worry, okay? You can put me in a cab from here."

"Charlie, if you really want to leave, I'll drive you to Mrs. Riley myself. . . . But do you think she could manage without you for a little while longer?" His voice was so low I had to lean in. "It would mean an awful lot to me if you stayed."

"You want me to stay?" I cried. Then I lowered my voice, trying not to sound eager. "You're sure I'm no trouble, Groover?"

"Believe me, Charlie," he said. "You're no trouble at all."

I swallowed hard and promised myself I'd never make him feel bad again.

"Thanks, Groover," I said. "And you don't have to worry about me overstaying my welcome. Just say the word and I'm out of here."

He seemed to wince. Clutching my suitcase in his arms, like it was all he had in the world, he carried it back upstairs.

EIGHT

That afternoon, I watched the soaps. But for the first time I was sitting on a sofa instead of in a closet. It was hard to keep my mind on other people's problems when I was worrying about Groover. Mother Superior was upset with Melissa, although I didn't know why yet 'cause I'd missed several days. And Doctor Tom's gold-digger girlfriend was already cheating on him with another man. Funny how some people get more pleasure being mean than nice.

During a break, I was about to get a Dr. Pepper, but a commercial stopped me. I suppose I'd seen it before, or something like it, but this time the words hit me like a punch in the stomach.

"Do you or someone you care about have a drinking problem?" a kind voice asked.

By the time the commercial ended, I was crying. *Does Groover have a drinking problem? Is that why he was staring at the bottle? What if he ends up like the derelict I'd seen, drinking whiskey from a paper bag?* A telephone number appeared at the bottom of the screen. Afraid I'd forget it by the time I found a pencil, I copied it in the dust on an end table. I stared at it for so long dust motes began to fill in the numbers like falling snow.

Later, I watched Groover from the front window. When he finished working on a car and went into the shop, I raced next door to Roberta's. I just knew she'd be happy to call the number for me, so we could figure out what to do about Groover.

I lifted the brass knocker on her door. Then I remembered her anger when she found the whiskey in the refrigerator. *Does she already know he has a problem? Will they get mad at each other again? What if they have a big fight? It will be all my fault.* Gently, I released the knocker. *I can't tell Roberta the truth,* I thought. *It might only make everything worse.*

I almost stumbled off the stoop when the door flew open.

"Charlie, you caught me on my way to work. Sorry I have no time to visit." Buttoning her coat, she stepped outside and closed the door. "Thanks for inviting me last night," she said. "It was really special. How's Uncle Grumpy today?"

"Groover? How is he? . . . He's good. Honest!"

She looked at me strangely. I forced my cold face into a smile. Frowning, Roberta glanced at her watch. "Anything you need to talk about, honey?"

"Nope. Everything's great. Never better."

My heart froze when she slipped the key in the lock. "Wait!" I cried.

She stared at me, puzzled.

"Roberta, could I borrow your phone? Groover doesn't have one, and I have to call Mrs. Riley, the lady who takes care of me."

She had the key off the ring before I finished my sentence. "You keep this one, I have a spare," she said. She started toward the car, then turned. Again she studied my face. "You sure nothing is wrong, Charlie?"

I nodded, afraid my voice would give me away.

"Go in before you get cold," she said, sliding into the car.

Once she pulled away, I rushed inside and dialed the number. My heart trembled in my throat when a voice answered. The woman gave me information and other phone numbers. After lots of calls, I knew what I had to do for Groover. Just the thought of it sent shivers up my spine.

Groover came out of the garage and spotted me walking away from Roberta's.

"Hi, Groover. I knocked and knocked, but Roberta didn't answer."

"Her car is gone," he said. "She's probably at work."

"Oh!" I gaped at the street, trying to look surprised that the car wasn't there. Lies sure have a way of multiplying.

"You feel all right, Charlie? You look a little funny."

"I feel great," I said. Avoiding his eyes, I held my hand out to catch snow flurries. "Do you think we'll get snow, Groover? A blizzard would be great, wouldn't it? Maybe I should get that sled down from the attic."

"I'll be through here in a minute," he called as I hurried away.

"That's okay. I'll get it."

I didn't expect it to snow. I just wanted to hide from Groover's watchful eyes so he wouldn't get suspicious. I couldn't let anything ruin my plan for late that night.

In the attic, I teetered carefully across the narrow boards like a tightrope walker. I figured it wouldn't improve my chances of staying with Groover if I crashed through the ceiling like an avalanche.

I poked through boxes in a large trunk, dragging clothing out. I tried on a dusty old hat. It slid down to my nose, and I sneezed six times in a row. I held dresses against myself that were much too long. They didn't have labels, and I wondered if Aunt Viola had made them.

Digging deeper into the trunk, I spied photographs that had spilled from a crushed box. I stared at one, unable to believe my eyes. It was a picture of me, but I'd never owned such clothes. My knees felt wobbly. Did I have a twin sister? I sat on the floor, the box of photographs in my lap.

Tears welled in my eyes as I sorted through them. I didn't have a sister, but I understood how Groover had recognized me immediately. My mother had even worn her brown hair in bangs like mine. The boyhood pictures of Groover made me laugh. In one he was holding up two fingers behind his sisters' heads, so they'd look like little devils.

Poor Aunt Viola. I loved her so much at that moment I almost cried. Not one photograph showed her smiling. But they showed the ragged clothes they all wore, clothes that had driven Aunt Viola to a sewing machine while her younger sister and brother skated under the moon. Being poor must have been so hard on her as a little girl, all these years later she would still rather be rich than happy.

Looking for more photographs, I found a high school yearbook. "Oh, gosh," I whispered, stopping at a page. I swept my hair on top of my head and lifted my chin. Would I ever become as beautiful as my mother? At the bottom of her picture, it said things like "great actress" and "loves to dance." I didn't think I could act, but it made me so happy that I might have her dancing-feet genes.

The name under another photo brought tears to my eyes. "Hi, Daddy," I whispered. No one had ever told me my parents went to the same high school. My father had a cowlick like mine. I patted it gently with my finger.

I bet he was the cutest boy in the whole graduating class. Reading the comments under his name, I knew I hadn't gotten any of his genes. My father, Michael Dearborn, wanted to be a sculptor. Under his picture, it said his statues would be famous worldwide.

Groover's picture was in a different yearbook. He was older than my mother and father. His smile was big, eyes bright. He was the senior class president, expected to go to college and become a professor.

I put the yearbooks back in the trunk. Empty picture frames were stacked on the floor beside it. Had Groover once intended to frame his family photographs? I wondered. *Had the thought slipped away like his dreams?* Before I left the attic, I piled the cartons of photographs beside the dusty frames.

• • •

The lie I told that night tasted sour, but I didn't know what else to do. "Groover, is it okay if I go to bed early tonight? I'm kind of tired from our New Year's Eve party." I opened my mouth, yawning loudly.

In my room, I dressed warmly, then puffed pillows under my blanket until it looked like I was in bed sound asleep. Layers of paint made it hard to open the window. I broke two pencils scraping it away. At last, I pried the window open and climbed into the tree. I hung onto a branch in an icy gust of wind. My fingers were almost numb when I finally reached the ground.

I crept on my toes through the backyard. Then I ran as fast as I could.

If I hadn't leaped out of the way at the corner, Joey's bicycle would have run me down.

"What are you doing out?" he asked.

"You're supposed to have lights on at night," I said nervously. "And what are you doing out?"

"I asked you first," he said.

"I'm going to church," I answered. "Where are you going?"

"No place," he said. "I just didn't feel like being home."

I thought about his mean father. If I were Joey, I guess I'd rather be out in the cold, too. He rode his bicycle beside me. He kept pace with me, but I wouldn't look at him, afraid he'd ask more questions.

"Want a lift?" he asked.

"No thank you. St. William's isn't very far."

"It is so," he said, stopping his bike. "The Catholic church is eight blocks from here."

I hadn't known it was so far away. Already I was shivering in the cold.

"Hop on," he said, turning the front wheel toward me. I eyed the rusty handlebars, wondering if they'd hold me. Gingerly, I climbed on. Joey huffed and puffed all the way to the church, but he didn't let me fall.

He pulled up to the stone steps that led to wide wooden doors.

"Want me to come in with you?" he asked shyly.

"No!" I cried, although I was frightened and wished he could come with me. But I didn't want Joey to see the terrible people I thought were inside. And I didn't want him thinking bad of Groover.

Joey looked hurt, then angry. "I'm glad I'm Lutheran!" he muttered, pedaling away. I didn't tell him that the people I was looking for weren't necessarily Catholic. They only rented rooms at churches and schools.

It was warm inside, and candles in glass jars flickered blue and red in front of the saints. I listened but couldn't hear voices. On the altar, the baby Jesus was lying in a manger, surrounded by animals and his mother. St. Joseph's plaster nose was chipped off. Still, they looked like a nice family.

"Where is everybody?" I whispered.

Disappointed, I went outside and circled the church. Something rustled under a pile of dead leaves. I tiptoed by. At the bottom of the basement stairs, an edge of light leaked around the door. I crept down the stairs, walked along a hallway, and pressed my ear to the first door. Hearing voices, I jumped back. Were the people inside dangerous? Would they let me stay? It didn't matter. I had nowhere else to turn. I took a deep breath, then plowed through the door before I lost my courage.

"Hi everyone! I'm here for the meeting of Alcoholics Anonymous!"

At first there wasn't a sound in the room. Everyone

was too busy staring at me to say a word. And I was staring at them. The men and women in the room couldn't be alcoholics. I thought alcoholics looked like the derelict at the train station. These people were dressed in nice clothes. And not one was drinking whiskey from a paper bag. Near the coffee urns, I recognized several people I'd seen in neighborhood stores. The AA meeting must have been canceled. Would there ever be another? The woman on the phone had told me that people with an alcohol problem went to Alcoholics Anonymous. If I didn't find out what they did about their problem, how would I learn how to help Groover?

"I guess I came to the wrong place," I murmured, turning toward the door.

Then two voices called out my name. "Charlie!"

The man who'd called me had thick white hair, his black eyebrows curling over his eyes like fringe. His suit and pinstripe shirt looked expensive, as nice as Uncle Ed's. I recognized him right away. It was Harry, Groover's friend who had stopped by the garage. Instead of walking toward me, he pointed at the woman who was hurrying across the room.

"Roberta!" I cried. "What are you doing here?"

Out of breath, she said, "The question is, what are *you* doing here, honey?"

I was too flustered to think of a lie, but I didn't mention Groover. "I'm looking for an AA meeting, Roberta.

There's supposed to be one around here. Can you help me find it? I need some information. It's . . . it's real important."

"This is the AA meeting, Charlie."

"It is?" Chairs scraped as people settled around a long table at the back of the hall. Near the coffee urn, Harry was still watching me. "You mean, you're . . . ?"

"An alcoholic? I sure am, honey."

Smiling, she slipped my hat off and scratched my head, fluffing up my hair. We sat down on two wooden chairs near the door.

"I didn't think you'd ever be an alcoholic, Roberta."

"Well, that makes two of us," she said with a laugh. Her face turned serious. She lowered her voice because the meeting was starting. "Why are you looking for AA, honey?"

I held my breath, holding in Groover's secret as well as my tears.

Roberta's eyes filled with concern. "Charlie? What is it?"

The tears I'd been holding in burst out. "It's . . . it's . . ."

"It's Groover!" she yelled, then lowered her voice quickly as people turned. "He got drunk, didn't he? I swear—"

"That's a helpful response," Harry said, his voice surprising both of us. He handed Roberta her coat. "Thought you might be needing this."

He patted my tears with a white handkerchief, his

bushy eyebrows frowning over kind eyes. "Does your uncle know you're out alone, Charlie?"

"Groover got drunk, Harry," Roberta said, tears welling in her eyes.

"But he didn't drink!" I said. "It's the way he was staring at the whiskey bottle. It really scared me and—"

Roberta jumped up, jamming her arm into her coat sleeve. "That man! I'm going over there and—"

"There's some rope in my trunk," Harry said, sighing patiently. "You want to tie him up and drag him to the meeting?"

Her shoulders slumped as she dropped back into the seat. Looking tired, she finally whispered, "Oh, I know, I know. There's not a darn thing we can do."

"There is so!" I insisted, starting to cry again. "I'll stay at the meeting, and you two can teach me how to make sure he never drinks, and I'll empty the bottle down the drain and—"

"Oh, sweetie." She pulled me into her arms and held me till I was all cried out. "You don't need AA, honey. You need some hot chocolate and someone to talk to."

I tried one last time. "How about this, Harry? I'll tell Groover I saw you here and that you really want him to come to a meeting 'cause . . . 'cause lots of people he knows here have car trouble and need to talk to him about it. When he gets here you can make him not want to drink whiskey!"

He rested his hand on my shoulder. "Charlie, listen to me. We can't trick Groover into coming to AA meetings or into not drinking. He has to want it. Understand? That's how it works."

I pulled my hat back on, yanking it low to avoid his eyes. I didn't want to hear what he was saying.

Gently, he lifted my chin. "And you don't want to be telling anyone, not even Groover, who you saw at this meeting," he added kindly. "Folks here have nothing to hide, but it's a matter of privacy. If we want someone to know we're sober in Alcoholics Anonymous, *we* tell them. Nobody else does the telling for us."

My eyes filled with tears again. "But if you don't tell Groover you're in AA, how will he know you have a problem like his? How will he know where to come?"

He glanced at Roberta, and I sensed there was something they weren't telling me. "Groover already knows I'm in AA, Charlie. Your uncle and I go back a long way." He gave my teary face another handkerchief pat and walked us outside to Roberta's car.

Roberta leaned up and kissed his cheek. "I'm okay now," she murmured. "I'll take it from here."

An old truck, belching white smoke, swerved into the space next to Roberta's car. The young man who hopped out had red high-top sneakers like mine. "Hi guys," he said. "Surprised to see you late for a meeting, Harry."

"I'm not late, Rudy. You are," Harry said.

"Well, I finally did it, Harry. Got my own business

going." He pointed to the bright lettering on the truck: Rudy's Rubbish Removal.

"Congratulations, Rudy," Harry said, smiling warmly. Then he leaned in for a closer look at the sign. "No job too *gross*?" he read.

"Yeah, what's wrong with that? I plan on cornering the rubbish market. So who's this?" he asked, grinning at me.

"This is Charlie, Groover's niece," Roberta said.

"Glad to meet you, Charlie. Is Groover already inside? It's about time that knucklehead came back to meetings!"

"Came back to meetings?" I said, smiling. "You mean Groover is in AA already?"

"Oops," Rudy said. "I guess she didn't know."

"Well, she knows now," Harry said. "You want to stand out here and break anyone else's anonymity, Rudy, or you want to come inside with me?"

Rudy smiled. "You're so judgmental, Harry. You should really work on that. I like your sneakers, Charlie," he said with a wink, making Harry roll his eyes.

"Thanks. I like your sign." Turning to Harry, I said, "You know what? My Uncle Ed has a suit just like yours. Are you the president of AA?"

"Hah!" Roberta hooted, walking around to the driver's side. "AA doesn't have a president," she said. "If it did, *I'd* be the president, not Harry."

"God help us all," Harry muttered, slamming my door.

Watching Harry and Rudy walk back to the meeting, I imagined the whiskey gurgling down the drain, flowing out to sea, and leaving Groover behind, safe with his friends. And happy forever with me.

. . .

I sank into Roberta's sofa cushions, setting my empty cup on the coffee table. The bay window was filled with hanging plants. The leaves of a prayer plant were folded together for the night. Cactus plants were in full bloom. But the Christmas tree had been taken down, the decorations put away.

My marshmallow mustache tasted sweet as I licked my lip clean. Roberta had listened to me without interruption.

"I'm really sorry I asked to live with him, Roberta. It must have been the thought of being stuck with me that made Groover think about drinking again."

Roberta was shaking her head even before I finished. "It's not your fault, honey, believe me. I can tell you that from personal experience. It's been a long time since I had my last drink, but the thought of a drink still enters my mind now and then. And it has nothing to do with good news or bad news or anything that's going on in my life. The reason I think about drinking sometimes is because I'm an alcoholic. And the reason I go to AA meetings is so I'll never forget it."

I guess Roberta wanted Groover to go back to meetings so he wouldn't forget he was an alcoholic either.

"Nothing you did or said made Groover think about drinking," she said. "Don't you feel the least bit responsible for that. Besides, he had that bottle in the house before you showed up."

"But he just bought it, remember? In case his friends stopped by for a drink around the holidays."

"I know Groover said that's why he bought it, and maybe he even believes it. But that bottle is in the house for only one person, honey. I wish I could tell you differently."

I pictured the terrible look in Groover's eyes as he stared at that bottle of whiskey. And I knew she was right.

"What'll we do, Roberta? There must be something."

"I don't think there's anything we can do, Charlie." She hugged a throw pillow to her chest. "It took Groover a few years to quit drinking after the—" Her eyes shifted away from me for a moment. "Well, it took him a while, that's all. But he's been sober now for over six years. Although you wouldn't know it from the looks of that house of his." She hugged the pillow tighter. "I wonder sometimes if Groover thinks he doesn't deserve a nice home. Doesn't deserve happiness and love . . . or forgiveness."

"What does he need forgiveness for, Roberta?"

She stared at me intensely, then shook her head. "Maybe that's something you should discuss with him, honey."

I thought of Aunt Viola's anger. Had he done something to hurt her?

"I wouldn't care what Groover did," I said. "I'd forgive him for anything."

"I'm sure you would, Charlie. Trouble is, Groover needs to forgive himself."

She reached out and pulled me close. "Don't give up on your uncle, honey. He might work through this yet. I bet a few prayers will help him a whole lot more than my big mouth. I'm working on keeping my mouth shut, Charlie. It's my biggest shortcoming."

She stood and put her hands on her hips. "Now what are we doing about you?"

"I'll climb back up the tree," I said.

"I have a better idea. Groover's place is dark. He must be asleep already. Spend the night with me. Tomorrow morning it might be a good idea for you and Groover to talk."

I followed her up the stairs. First she got me a long pajama top, then a new toothbrush and fresh towel.

When I finished undressing, she was waiting in the hallway in front of a closed door. She reached for the knob, hesitated, then opened the door, flicking on a light switch.

"You can sleep in here," she said softly.

My red sneakers sunk into a plush white carpet. There was a single bed in the room. The bedspread was pink with frilly ruffles along the bottom. There was a pink canopy over the bed, like something a princess might have. A stuffed dog rested against a pillow. The room was bathed in a soft pink glow from the lamp on the night table. The light picked up the wetness in Roberta's eyes.

"You had a little girl?" I whispered.

"I did, honey. She went and got sick on me. After we lost her, things fell apart with her father and me." She turned down the blanket and sheet. "He got married again though. He has a couple of kids now."

"How come you never married again?" I asked.

"I've had my eye on someone, Charlie. But he's not ready for me yet."

She winked at me and I grinned.

We sat on the bed, and she picked up a framed picture of a little girl, her hair as red as Roberta's. Sighing, she stared at the photograph. "My Mary was a funny little thing, Charlie. From the time she could talk, she made me laugh. I think she would have grown up to be a lot like you. Sometimes I still can't believe she's gone."

She put the frame down, smacked her knees hard, and stood. At the door, she paused, watching me in her daughter's bed. I hoped she wasn't sorry for letting me stay. When she closed the door, I hugged the plush dog in my arms and prayed as hard as I could.

NINE

THE NEXT MORNING I SLIPPED into the house early. I didn't tell Groover I'd been to an AA meeting. And I didn't tell him I was worried about the way he'd stared at the bottle of whiskey. He'd gotten up in such a good mood, I didn't want to say anything to spoil it. That afternoon, he hid in the garage, working on a surprise for me. Once I tried to peek through the door, but he blocked my view, his eyes bright with mischief. It was impossible to believe Groover needed to be forgiven for anything.

"How long do I have to wait?" I cried. "Can't I have a hint?"

Suddenly the door burst open, and Groover rode out on a girl's two-wheeler. Playing cards were attached to the metal spokes with clothespins. The wheels went *ticka, ticka, ticka* as he pedaled around me.

Smiling, he hopped off and leaned the bicycle toward me. "Merry late-Christmas," he said.

Trying hard to smile, I said, "Thanks, Groover. It's a good surprise."

His excitement made him look like the boy in the yearbook. The bike was secondhand, but there were new strips of purple plastic streaming from the handlebars. And he'd put a furry cover on the seat. I patted it gently.

"Give it a try," he said. I didn't move.

Slowly, Groover's enthusiasm drained away. He stuffed his hands in his pockets. "I know it's not as good as the bike you must have, Charlie, but I thought you'd like one while you're here. It used to be your mother's."

"It's a great bike, Groover. Honest." I stepped over the low bar in front of the seat, keeping my head down, and fingered the silver bell, *ring, ring.* Snowflakes melted on my cheeks.

"Charlie?"

I looked into his eyes.

"Oh, Charlie," he whispered. "You don't know how to ride a bike?"

"They would have bought me one, Groover," I told him. "But see, there are so many hills . . ."

A flash of anger lit his eyes. "Well, there are no damn hills here," he muttered. "On the seat! Let's go."

"I can't!"

He slapped the seat, but his eyes were smiling again. "Up!" he ordered.

My feet were barely on the pedals when he started running, one hand on the back of the seat, the other on the handlebar.

He removed his hand from the front, and I shouted, "Don't let go!"

"I've got you!" Poor Groover. I could hear him keeping pace—*huff, huff, huff.* "You're . . . getting . . . it," he gasped, his feet slapping against the pavement while I pedaled for my life.

He must have run a mile with me, from one end of the block to the other. Then Roberta raced out of her house, and Groover groaned. She put her fingers between her teeth and gave a piercing whistle. "Hey Groov! Good thing you've been going to the gym every day!" (I guess she still needed work on her shortcoming.)

I could tell his teeth were gritted. "You're a riot, Roberta," he wheezed. She responded with hoots and more whistles.

Joey came flying down the street on his bike. He fell in beside us and didn't make fun that I couldn't ride. I figured learning to ride a bicycle might take forever, but I didn't care. Pedaling with Joey, while Groover ran behind—well, it was the best day of my life.

"Hold me tight, Groover!" I cried.

Standing on the pedals, Joey yelled over his shoulder, "Groover's not there anymore!"

"Groover!" I screamed. There was no answer. My front wheel wiggled so hard I almost lost balance. But my legs kept pumping, the wind and laughter bringing tears to my eyes. And I didn't get mad when Joey showed off, riding no-hands.

I made a wide turn to head back.

"You're doing great," Joey yelled.

In front of the house, Groover was still trying to catch his breath, his hands on his knees. Roberta was laughing so hard she had to lean on our picket fence. When Joey and I raced past them, my wheels going *ticka, ticka,* I rang my silver bell, over and over.

Roberta cheered, "Way to go, Charlie! Pick up an oxygen tank on the way back!" Then Groover couldn't help but laugh. I was so happy I caught snowflakes on my tongue—and almost drove Joey into a tree.

• • •

Snowflakes glittered in the glow of a streetlight and dusted the ground. I imagined a guardian angel sprinkling silver dust all around Groover's house, hiding the weeds and rusty engine parts until the outside looked as pure as Groover's heart. But not even a guardian angel could fly that whiskey bottle out of the house.

Some of the men I'd seen at the AA meeting stopped

by the garage, old friends who said they happened to be in the neighborhood. They never said a word about the bottle in the house. And they didn't tell Groover to come back to meetings. They were funny and friendly, though, and I could tell Groover liked them. Certainly they liked him, 'cause they kept showing up, and they didn't seem to mind the cold garage. Even Rudy stopped by once, winking at me, but pretending we'd never met. Groover laughed at the sign on the truck— NO JOB TOO GROSS—and said he'd think about the swap Rudy offered, an engine overhaul in exchange for cleaning up Groover's property.

More and more I worried about Aunt Viola's return. I didn't want Groover to know how she really felt about him. And more than anything, I didn't want to leave him. Sometimes I'd catch him watching me, and you would have thought he loved me so much he'd never let me go. But he didn't ask me to stay.

Joey came by after school one day. We went bike riding while Groover was at the store. At home with Mrs. Riley, I would have been going to school, too. I had a week before my aunt and uncle returned from Europe. I tried to keep Aunt Viola's face out of my mind. But it hit me full blast like the wind. What would she say when she found out what I'd done? How would Groover feel when he learned she didn't like him?

Joey let go of the handlebars. You should have seen him turn a corner without holding on. He was the best no-handed rider I ever saw. Would there be time enough for me to learn how to ride without hands? Near the house, a car horn blasted. It was Joey's father, driving the brown car.

"Get yourself home, boy," he snarled from the window. "You're supposed to be doing chores to pay off my car, not playing with girls like a sissy."

Startled, Joey drove up on the sidewalk and hit the tree in front of Groover's house. He lost balance and fell. His face bunched up like a fist, watching his father drive away.

"You okay, Joey?" I kicked the stand on my bike.

Not answering, he yanked his bike upright. The tire was flat, a spoke broken.

"Groover can fix it," I said.

"I don't want that old drunk touching my bike!" His face turned red with anger. I felt the heat rise in my own.

"And what are you doing here, anyway?" he shouted. "How can you live with someone who got drunk and killed both your parents?"

"You're a dirty liar!" My hand shot out and smacked his face.

The air went silent. The color drained from his skin, except for the red mark where I'd hit him. I started crying, wishing I could pull back my slap. Joey hung his head, and I think we both wished he could take back his words.

I heard Roberta calling out. "What's wrong, you guys?" I didn't wait for her to reach us. I turned and ran into the house. I locked the doors, front and back, so she couldn't get in. Then I raced up the stairs to pack.

I dragged a chair to a closet, searching for my suitcase. *Groover had killed my parents.* The suitcase wasn't there. Climbing down, I banged my shin and started crying. *Groover had killed my mother and father.* The words didn't seem real. They couldn't be real.

Where had Groover put my suitcase? The doorbell rang again and again. From the urgency, I knew it was Roberta. Joey must have told her what he'd said. Ignoring the bell, I continued to search, in the attic, under the bed, in every closet. I pushed hanging clothes aside, not caring that they fell to the floor.

Groover had killed my parents. That was all I could think about. I had to go away before he returned; I just had to. And it wasn't because I was mad at him. Or because I couldn't forgive him. It was only because I couldn't bear to see the pain on his face when he found out I knew the truth.

At the back of a walk-in closet, I came upon the packages, heaps and heaps of them, in all sizes, wrapped in brown paper. There were so many they could have filled a post office—the dead-letter drop, where mail stays lost forever. Every package was addressed to me, with my name crossed out, replaced by Aunt Viola's writing: "Return to Sender."

It seemed forever before I carried the last package into the bedroom. Inside the brown paper, the packages were wrapped again: Christmas paper, birthday paper, some covered with red Valentine hearts—and other gifts that seemed for no reason at all. My fingers fumbled with the wrapping. My throat ached as I peered inside the boxes: every doll I'd ever wanted, a sewing kit, tap shoes, a baseball and mitt; there were even tiny ice skates, and another pair like my mother's that would fit me now. That package had already been opened, an ice skate missing one blue pom-pom. I wound up a music box, and the carousel on top went round and round. This Christmas he'd sent a basketball. Unlike the Santa Claus who came to Aunt Viola's, Groover had always known what was on my list.

I was still opening presents when he entered the room. His face was pale, his eyes so deep I thought I'd fall into them and drown. He knelt in front of me.

"Oh, Charlie. Can you ever forgive me?"

I was shaking too hard to speak.

"I should have told you right away," he said. "I was wrong to keep such a thing from you." He pulled me close and pressed his face against my hair. I listened to his chest thumping in my ear.

"I'd just gotten out of the service. . . . I had a bad accident. . . . Oh, Charlie, I was *drunk*. That's the damn truth. I can't make it sound any better." He held me so tightly I could barely breathe. "Your mom and dad were coming to see me in the hospital. They wouldn't have been on that ferry but for me. Your aunt was right to keep us apart, Charlie, to tell me never to show my face at your door. I don't deserve to have you in my life."

Groover rocked me while I sobbed against his chest. The music ended, and the carousel horses stopped. I hugged him tighter, unable to let go. Groover thought I was crying because he had killed my parents. But I knew he had never meant to take them away from me. I stared at the gifts, my breath coming in gulps. I was crying because of Aunt Viola: *How could she have kept all that love from a little girl?*

TEN

THAT NIGHT I TOSSED SO MUCH I almost wore out the sheets. Hearing a floorboard creak below, I figured Groover couldn't sleep either. I jumped out of bed, scooped up unopened presents, and padded down the stairs.

Before he heard me, I watched him studying the living room like it was the first time he'd seen it. He folded some clothes, then stood there not knowing where to put them. He pulled a handkerchief from his pocket and started to wipe off the top of the piano. Sighing, he stuffed the handkerchief back in his pocket and tossed the clothes onto the sofa. I guess he knew that the house was such a mess he could never clean it alone.

"Hi, Groover," I said.

"Oh, hi, Charlie. Have trouble sleeping?"

"Maybe I could help you clean tomorrow," I said.

"I'd rather see you opening presents than cleaning this dump, Charlie. I don't know how it got so far away from me. It used to look pretty good."

"I guess you knew all along that I'd written that letter, huh."

His smile was tender. "Well, I knew my sister hadn't written it." He took the packages from me and placed them on the sofa.

"Maybe you should be mad at her, instead of the other way around."

"Don't be angry at your aunt, Charlie. She's not the one at fault. It was my drinking that cost you a wonderful mother and father."

"Is that why you didn't tell me about the presents, Groover? So I wouldn't be mad at Aunt Viola?"

"She felt responsible for you, Charlie. She was just doing what she thought was right. Think you can get over being mad at her?"

"I guess," I said, my voice still sulky.

Groover reached for a gift and shook it near my ear, smiling.

"What's clicking in here?" I said, tearing the paper off.

Groover wiggled his eyebrows. "I used to be a champion," he said.

"No way!" I cried, slapping the checkers on the board.

After the third game, Groover insisted I kept winning because black pieces were luckier, so we switched.

"How come people call you Groover?" I asked. "How come they don't call you . . . Chuck?" I jumped his black with my red.

"Chuck?" he repeated. He moved a piece. "Do me a favor, Charlie. Don't ever ask me that in front of Roberta. She'd be calling me Chuck forever."

I rubbed my hands briskly and jumped him three times in a row.

"I bet she'd be the perfect girlfriend for a person," I said. "King me."

He narrowed his eyes. "Charlie, I have enough trouble with checkers, without worrying about women. I'm called Groover," he stressed, "not Chuck, because of my father. Your grandfather."

"Did your father have . . . larceny in his heart?" I kept my eyes on the checkerboard.

He gave a short laugh. "Sounds like you've been talking to my sister. That's an old saying, Charlie. It means a person isn't completely honest or trustworthy."

I looked up guiltily.

Groover just smiled. "But I guess Pop did roll a few odometers back when he was selling cars: lower mileage meant higher prices. And he was a groover, no denying that."

"A groover?" I took three of his pieces.

"Lucky move," Groover snorted. "Pop grooved new

treads into bald tires; he burned them right into the rubber so the tires wouldn't look so old. He was always trying to make a buck, but it was dangerous letting folks drive on bad tires. Some of his friends in the car business knew he did it. When I was young, they used to ask, 'How's the little groover?' The name stuck. Everyone called me Groover, except for your aunt. She hated Pop's drinking and being poor. She hated my name. . . ." Idly, he rubbed the scar near his eye, the scar he'd gotten in the accident. "Eventually, I guess she hated me, too."

I rested my chin in my hands. "Joey was hateful today, Groover. I was really mean to him, too."

He tucked a strand of hair behind my ear. "Feelings have a way of taking over sometimes, Charlie. If we're not careful, they can turn us into someone we don't want to be."

I kept my eyes on him. "I guess we all have to forgive ourselves, huh, Groover?"

He became very still, as though playing my words over in his mind. Finally he said, "You know what, Charlie? I think you're absolutely right."

Smiling, I let him win the last game of checkers.

Afterward, I opened the rest of my gifts. Groover played the piano while I plinked a child's piano like the one in the Charlie Brown cartoons. A pair of tap shoes were much too small, but I wore them like gloves and clap-tapped to a ragtime tune.

Groover spun a yo-yo up and down. Suddenly he

hopped it just above the ground like a walking dog, then rocked it in the air like a baby's cradle.

I opened a box of clay. I liked the smell, sweet and earthy. I rolled a snake out on the coffee table, then balled the clay again. Out of nowhere I pictured Mrs. Rendlethorp's bug-eyed dog. Oddly, I could almost see the dog trapped inside the ball of clay. I pinched and pressed and pulled bits of clay away.

Groover stopped yo-yoing and watched me.

"That's a pug," he said in surprise.

"Our neighbor, Mrs. Rendlethorp, has one," I said.

"It's a perfect likeness."

I turned the dog head in my hands, smoothing out an ear. "It is pretty good, huh?" My drawings in art class were always good, but this was the first time I'd molded clay.

Groover reached for the bronze statue of the little girl and handed it to me.

"I'll never be this good, Groover. That's for sure."

"Your father made that, Charlie."

"He did? It's beautiful." I ran my fingers over the cold bronze. It gave me the good feeling I'd gotten the first time I touched it, when I had just arrived at Groover's house.

"He was a talented guy. . . . And pretty good at forging signatures in school, as I recall." I peeked up at Groover's face, but he wasn't looking at me. "Fortunately, he grew out of that and started sculpting."

"I don't think Aunt Viola liked my father or my mother," I said.

"Believe me, Charlie, she loved them both. But she didn't want your mother being poor."

"I wish she was more like Uncle Ed. He never worries about money."

"He never had to," Groover said gently.

"I'm sorry you and Aunt Viola don't get along, Groover."

"I'm sorry too, Charlie, believe me."

"At least we got to meet."

He nodded.

I spoke cautiously, remembering the bottle. "Too bad I have to go back to Connecticut . . . but that's life, right?"

"You're missing school," he said. The yo-yo trembled in the air, then rolled up slowly. Groover seemed lost in thought.

"I'm really smart, Groover. I'll catch up. We still have another week together," I said. My voice sounded small. "Maybe I could visit another time. Not for long, though. I won't be a bother."

The yo-yo slid up and down.

In a quiet voice he said, "Maybe we could go on vacation together someday."

My heart soared. "That's a great idea!"

"What's the name of that travel agent your aunt and uncle use?" he asked.

When I told him, he nodded, without meeting my

eyes. The yo-yo snapped into his hand.

• • •

He was gone the next morning before I got up, something he'd never done before.

The cupboard drew me like a magnet.

I stood in front of it, my heart beating in my throat. When I looked inside, the bottle was gone. I swung open the refrigerator door, but it wasn't there either. I searched the kitchen, cupboard to cupboard, but it was nowhere to be found. I ran out the back door and opened the garbage can. The whiskey bottle was inside. Only this time it was empty. Crying, I kicked the can so hard it toppled over. Why did Groover drink the whiskey? Was it the fear of being stuck with me? Then I remembered what Roberta had said: If Groover drinks, it's because he's an alcoholic. It has nothing to do with me.

All morning I watched the clock. Where had he gone? What if he never came back? I pounded the pug into a pancake, then rolled him into a snake.

Hearing a car crunch on the gravel, I rushed to the window. Groover was getting out of Harry's car, but he didn't look drunk or sad. He was smiling when Harry pulled away—*smiling*—and I realized he didn't drink that whiskey after all. He must have poured it down the drain. When he walked toward Roberta's, I ran outside to wait, trying to puff angel halos in the cold air.

I raced toward him when he finally came out. "Hi,

Groover. I wondered where you went this morning."

"I taped a note on the refrigerator, Charlie. Didn't you see it?"

I shook my head. "It's okay. I wasn't worried. Honest."

"I needed to . . . meet with some old friends of mine this morning."

"That's great!" I was grinning like crazy. "And how's Roberta?"

"Don't get any ideas, Charlie. I just needed to borrow her phone."

"Oh. Who were you calling?"

I thought his smile slipped a little.

But Joey walked up then, and Groover went into the garage without answering my question. When he wheeled Joey's bicycle out, I figured that's who he had called. Joey avoided my eyes at first, and when he did glance my way, I looked down. It was the first time we'd seen each other since he told me about my parents.

"Thanks for fixing the bike, Groover," he said shyly. "How much do I owe you?"

"That'll be two hundred and eighty dollars, Joey. And don't forget the tip."

Joey smiled self-consciously.

"Tell your father I have a car he might want to take a look at. It's old, but the engine is good."

Joey scuffed the ground with his shoe. "My father moved out," he said. "He and my mother . . . I guess they're getting a divorce."

I couldn't believe Joey would look so upset that his father was gone. But I guess he felt even a mean father was better than no father at all.

"Come on inside," Groover said gently, placing his arm across Joey's shoulder. "I owe you some money for the paper."

Joey's eyes shifted in my direction, but we both looked away quickly.

It's funny how words can get stuck in your throat, and all the wanting in the world won't shake them loose. I went over to my bicycle. I took the clothespins and cards off the spokes and walked to Joey's bike.

When he rode off, his wheels went *ticka, ticka, ticka.* I watched him leave, tears caught in my throat with all the words. Then he turned back. He popped a wheelie in front of the house. "You want to ride no-handed?" he called.

• • •

One day, Groover and I took a walk on a sandy beach near his house. For the first time, he told me he was an alcoholic and that alcoholism was a disease. He said sobriety had changed his life and that he'd be going back to AA meetings. The cold front had passed, leaving warmer air behind. His brown hair blew across his forehead as he stared at the bay. I'd never seen him so happy and content—except when he was looking at me.

"I forgot how much I loved the Great South Bay," he said. "I used to come out here every morning and walk, even in winter. For the last couple of years, I just got out of the habit. In the summertime, you can smell the marsh. Some people don't like the smell at low tide, but I love it. I wouldn't live anywhere else."

A brown dog bounded toward us. It pawed the sand in front of us, its tail wagging. It was a big dog, the kind I'd always wanted. Groover threw a stick, and the dog ran after it.

"Do you think that kind of dog sheds?" I asked. "Aunt Viola says they all shed."

"That's a chocolate Labrador retriever," he answered. "I used to have one."

"Really? Did it shed?"

He snugged my scarf a little tighter around my neck. "I never noticed."

Smiling, he looked back at the bay. The retriever dropped the stick at my feet, sat down, and seemed to grin at me. Before I could throw it, a man whistled and the dog ran off. One of my presents had been a Frisbee. We could play catch on the sand, I thought, me and a dog and Groover. If only I didn't have to leave.

Groover looked at his watch.

"Rudy is coming over with a bunch of the guys," he said. "They're probably at the house already."

"That's great!"

He slipped my gloved hand into his pocket, holding

it tightly as we walked back to the car. He didn't start the engine. We sat there together, listening to the sea gulls. He seemed so happy to be with me, all the hope I'd tried to hold back rushed into my heart.

A moment later, my dreams of a life with Groover ended.

"Charlie, there's something we have to talk about," he said.

I waited.

"Your aunt and uncle are coming tomorrow."

They're not due back yet," I cried. "And how do they know I'm here?"

"I called the travel agency, Charlie. They contacted—"

"That's not fair!" I cried. "I still have time left!"

"Charlie, listen to me—"

"I won't listen to you!"

He had thrown out the bottle of whiskey, and now all he cared about was a stinky old marsh and his friends.

"I hate you!" I sobbed. "I'm *glad* I'm going back. Your house is like a barn. I'd never want to live with you. Not in a million years!"

"Let me explain—"

"You don't know *anything* about a home." My body was shaking, and he tried to hold me. I pulled away. "All your photographs are stuck in boxes in a musty old attic. Photographs are supposed to be in frames! When you love somebody, if you *really* love them, you want to see them every day."

Before he could stop me, I jumped from the car and ran. I heard him calling my name, but I didn't stop. Sobbing, my breath almost froze in my chest. My sneakers pounded the sidewalk. I heard his car backfire and ducked around the corner. I kept going, without looking back.

Gasping for breath, I stood in front of St. William's. I raced up the steps. The church was silent and empty. I approached the saint who had his arm around a child. In front of the statue, candles flickered as though leaning away from me. Harshly, I blew out the flames, row after row, until all that was left were curls of black smoke.

"So there!" I yelled at the saint.

ELEVEN

THE SUN SET BEHIND A stained-glass window, brilliant reds and blues shimmering around a white dove. I sat alone in the quiet church for hours, long after my anger was gone. Soon it would get dark, and I knew I had to go back. A priest came through a side door near the altar. I was about to say hello when he stopped in front of the saint with the blown-out candles. I heard him grumble in annoyance. Quickly, I hid but peeked over the back of the pew and watched him empty the money boxes under the candles by the different saints. The colors died in the windows as darkness fell. Finally, the priest left.

I hurried toward the door, knowing Groover would be worried. He must have really wanted to get rid of me if he sent for Aunt Viola and Uncle Ed. Still, I didn't want him being upset that I was out after dark. I felt awful for running off and for the terrible things I'd said, too. And I felt awful because he didn't want me.

At the back of the church, I pulled on the door handle. It didn't budge. Thinking it was jammed, I pushed and pulled even harder. The door wouldn't open. I realized the priest had locked it when he left. I raced up the aisle to the side door that the priest had first come through. It was locked too. Oh, no, I thought. Groover will think I've run away.

I pounded on the door, over and over. "Hello, hello. Anybody out there?"

My words echoed in the empty church.

There was nothing I could do until the priest came back and unlocked the door. Crying, I curled up on a hard pew, my hands in prayer under my head for a pillow. I didn't mean to fall asleep. I dreamed that the white dove broke free of the blood-red window, its cry the tinkle of shattered glass. I dreamed about the mean things I'd said to Groover.

When I opened my eyes, it was morning. The sun was behind a stained-glass angel with eyes so bright she seemed to be watching me like a guardian angel. "Well you didn't do a very good job," I said. Her eyes flashed back in the sunlight.

Suddenly, I heard someone hurrying up the aisle. Then Roberta slid into my pew, out of breath.

"Hi, Roberta," I whispered.

"Hi'ya, Charlie." She pulled me into her arms. "You must be as stiff as a board."

"I got locked in," I said. "And I had a big fight with Groover yesterday."

"I know, honey. He searched for you all afternoon while Rudy and the guys stayed at the house in case you came back. Joey's mom thought the two of you had gone off somewhere together, but it turned out he was at the movies. Once it got dark . . . well, you can imagine how worried we were. We had to call the police."

"How'd you know I was here?"

"There's an early morning AA meeting downstairs," she answered. "After the meeting, I was halfway to the car when I saw the priest unlock the church. I can't explain it, Charlie, but this urge to make a visit came over me. And there you were."

I peeked over my shoulder at the angel in the stained-glass window.

"I called Groover from the pay phone when I found you sleeping. He's one relieved uncle, honey."

"How'd you call him? He doesn't have a phone?"

"He'd arranged to have his turned back on. It was working first thing this morning. How about I drive you back, Charlie?"

"I said the meanest things yesterday, Roberta. I bet Groover's mad at me."

"That's a bet you'll lose, honey. There was something he didn't get to tell you yesterday. He sent for your aunt and uncle because he'd like you to live with him."

"He wants me?" I whispered.

"Like you wouldn't believe," she said. "There's one problem, Charlie. Your aunt's not too happy with Groover. He figures she's going to try and keep you two apart. And he doesn't want you being mad at her. But he made up his mind to try and make things work. Assuming you want to live with him, of course." She laughed at the look in my eyes. "The Judge is coming over this morning to give him a hand with your aunt."

Before we left, I remembered the candles I'd blown out. Roberta helped me light them again. In fact, she insisted we light every candle—because the saint liked children.

"Don't we have to leave money for lighting the extra candles?" I asked.

"It's okay, Charlie," she said. "My Higher Power lets me run a tab."

"My aunt's going to be really mad, Roberta. You should see how nice her house is. And my bedroom always has to be neat. She might take me away, and I'll never see Groover again."

"Maybe she'll bend a little, honey."

"*Snap* is more like it," I said.

Roberta stared at the child with the saint. Her eyes glistened, and she seemed lost in thought. Then she nodded her head as though making a decision.

Leaving church, she held my hand tightly. "Charlie, I have to give Rudy a quick call. I need some work done in a hurry. If it's not too late. Then how about we grab breakfast before going back? Rudy can tell your uncle."

I blinked my eyes in the daylight. The air smelled of winter and snow and the salty bay. *Groover wanted me with him.* I tried not to think about Aunt Viola's reaction. I tried not to picture her face when she saw the condition of Groover's house. All my presents were out and looked nice, but that old iron bed . . . In my mind, her dark eyebrows snapped together, her lips tightened. I hope Groover got a Supreme Court judge, I thought.

Roberta was very quiet at the diner. Once she reached over and brushed back a strand of my hair. After breakfast, we took a long walk on the beach. I wanted so much to see Groover. But I was afraid it might be the last time I'd ever see him.

A duck floated on the bay, looking cold and alone.

Driving back, we saw Rudy in his truck with two other men. He tooted the horn and gave us a thumbs-up. I figured he was just wishing us luck.

When we turned the corner, I saw the Cadillac Seville pulling up in front of the house. I squeezed my eyes shut and slid down in the seat, my hopes sliding down with me. Aunt Viola would never let me stay with Groover. One look at the house— and I'd be on my way back to Connecticut.

I opened one eye when Roberta turned off the engine. We were in her driveway.

"Are you coming with me?" I asked.

"Honey, the *last* thing this situation needs is my big mouth," she said. She pressed her hands to my cheeks. "Think good thoughts, Charlie. And good things will come back to you." She gave me a big hug, smoothed my hair, and sent me on my way.

Walking toward the house, I kept my eyes squinty to avoid seeing Aunt Viola clearly. But they opened wide when she let out a shriek.

"Would you look at her? Look at her, Edward," she said, poking him. Uncle Ed rolled his eyes at me, but knew better than to smile. "Three weeks and she looks like an urchin. Charlotte Dearborn . . ." She shook her head in exasperation, releasing a stream of cold air.

I'd forgotten about my red high-top sneakers and my new Wal-Mart clothes.

"Hello, Aunt Viola," I said. "Did you have a lovely time in Europe?"

"Don't you *Aunt Viola* me," she snapped. "Look at yourself, young lady."

I scanned the street, wishing Groover's judge would hurry up.

Groover was still inside. I'd been so focused on Aunt Viola I hadn't even noticed the house. Looking around, I felt like I was dreaming. The windows were sparkling. The hinge on the gate was repaired, the yard cleaned up. Even the fence had been painted white. The house still needed a coat of paint, but it didn't look abandoned anymore. You could tell it was somebody's home. Groover's friends must have worked on the house all afternoon while he searched for me.

Finally Groover stepped onto the porch. His hair was parted and combed to the side. He wore a sports jacket and white shirt. He nervously smoothed his tie down, but it blew over his shoulder again. Frosty air puffed from his mouth. I figured he was cold without his warm winter jacket. But I guess he wanted Aunt Viola to see how nice he could look.

She stiffened at his approach. Uncle Ed hummed softly.

Suddenly, Groover spotted me. He looked toward Roberta's house and saw her at the front door. His face softened, and he gave her a slight nod. She nodded back, then went inside.

Groover hurried toward me, his eyes steady but tired. He spoke so no one could hear.

"Everything okay, Charlie? You had me worried to death."

"Everything's good with me, Groover. Except for the mean things I said yesterday. I'm really sorry."

"Yesterday was yesterday, Charlie. Can we start all over?"

He didn't have to ask me twice.

He lowered his voice even more. "Have I read things right, Charlie? You'd really like to live with me?"

"Are you sure you want me, Groover?" I whispered.

Smiling, he pressed my bangs down with his big hand, and they lengthened over my eyes.

Then he took a deep breath and faced his sister. "Hello, Vi," he said. "You're looking great."

"Her new coat's exquisite, isn't it?" I said. I backed away from her glare.

Groover and Uncle Ed shook hands warmly. "Hey, Eddie. Good to see you."

"Likewise," Uncle Ed said.

"Still like those stogies, I see."

"I'm quitting," Uncle Ed muttered around the dead cigar.

Aunt Viola took charge. "Charlotte, get your things. We're leaving."

"Let's talk about this, Vi," Groover said.

"There's nothing to talk about, Charles. This girl is not living like a pauper. Not knowing where the next meal is coming from. Dressed like . . . " She pointed at me. " . . . like a ragpicker."

"She looks okay to me," Uncle Ed said, under his breath.

"I bet that house is a shambles inside," Aunt Viola added. "I won't have her ashamed to bring her friends home. I won't have people making fun of her at school. Never again, do you hear me. Never!" I remembered the photographs of Aunt Viola when she'd been poor. I knew she was thinking of her own childhood, as much as mine.

Groover stepped closer.

"It won't be like that, Vi—"

Everyone turned when the car pulled up.

"That's Harry Bender," Groover said. "I asked him to—"

"Harold Bender!" Aunt Viola interrupted. "I heard he became a judge. Well, you can invite all the judges you want. They don't frighten me."

A white-haired man lumbered from the front seat. His black eyebrows curled over his eyes like fringe. It was Harry from the AA meeting.

His eyes twinkled as he placed his finger under my chin to close my mouth.

"I didn't know you were a judge, Harry," I said.

"Don't think your black robes are going to impress me," Aunt Viola said. "You threw spitballs in school. And I'm sure you're no better now."

"Viola, it's a pleasure to see you again." He was extra polite, but Aunt Viola squinted suspiciously, as though expecting a spitball to fly from his mouth.

"This girl is coming right back to Connecticut," Aunt Viola said. "You can smack that gavel all you want."

"I'm not here to smack any gavels, Vi. Groover is a good friend of mine. He asked me to stop by."

Aunt Viola looked surprised. I guess she didn't expect Groover to have a friend with a nice car who was a judge. But Harry's words felt like a lump of hard clay in my stomach. If a judge didn't force Aunt Viola to give Groover custody of me, I knew there was no way she'd let me stay.

"Shall we discuss this inside?" he said. "Or am I the only one who's freezing?"

"Let's stay out here!" I cried, thinking of the messy house. "I'll run in and get your jacket, Groover!"

But Aunt Viola pushed through the gate, the new hinges swinging it shut against her backside.

"I'm getting your belongings out of this pigsty, Charlotte. I'm sure even this judge wouldn't let you live in here."

As she marched away we all stared at the wet paint stripes across her new coat.

Judge Harry sighed patiently. Groover gave him a sheepish grin.

When we caught up to Aunt Viola in the living room, her mouth could have caught flies—mine, too. A prayer plant like Roberta's sat on the coffee table. The piano glistened. The air smelled of lemon wax. Groover's bedding was gone from the sofa. There wasn't a dust bunny in the whole room.

But that wasn't the most amazing thing: Every photograph from the attic was in a frame. They were on the piano, the coffee table, the ledge of the bay window, and hanging on every wall. Honestly, it took all my control not to throw myself into Groover's arms.

Aunt Viola scratched away a price tag that was still glued in the corner of a frame. I thought she would criticize Groover for being careless, but she never said a word. She was staring at the photograph of Groover, his fingers raised behind his sisters' heads.

She looked up the stairs toward my bedroom.

"Well, that's the house," I cried, swinging the front door wide. "How about we sit on the porch and chat?" I couldn't let Aunt Viola see my bedroom. One look at the faded curtains, the iron folding bed, why I'd never be allowed to stay with Groover.

Harry gave me a Supreme Court frown. He closed the door against the cold wind.

My heart sank as I followed Aunt Viola up the stairs. Groover's bedroom door was slightly ajar. I peeked in as we passed and saw his bed made, the blanket folded down over fresh sheets.

Cringing, I joined Aunt Viola in my bedroom. The iron bed was gone, and so was the ripped blanket. My stuffed animals and baby dolls were arranged on the new bed. I gazed in amazement, feeling like I'd been magically beamed into Roberta's house. My feet sunk into the plush white carpet. I ran my fingers along the pink bedspread—and the canopy that a princess might have. I went to the window and pushed the pink curtains aside. I saw Roberta watching from her house.

I remembered telling her in church that Aunt Viola might take me away from Groover because my bedroom always had to be neat. I remembered her face as she stared at the statue of the child, and the tenderness in her eyes when she looked at me. Now I knew what she'd asked Rudy to do. I pressed my forehead against the clean window, the breath from my nose puffing tiny angel wings on the cold glass. She smiled and toodle-ooed with her fingers—from her daughter's empty bedroom.

Behind me, I heard the others enter the room.

Aunt Viola seemed surprised at the bedroom, but her voice was still stern. "A nice room isn't enough, Charles! She's not going to live with a . . . a *drunk*, do you hear me. Shame on you for even suggesting it."

"I haven't had a drink in six years, Vi!"

"And I'm supposed to believe that!"

"You read my letter five years ago, telling you I hadn't had a drink in a year! Why couldn't you have trusted me enough to find out if it was true? You would have seen that I was staying sober all these years if you'd let me visit—"

"What are you talking about? I never read any letter. You know very well I sent them back." She looked at Uncle Ed for confirmation, and he nodded.

"You did read the letter," Groover insisted. "I told you how sorry I was about everything I'd done and that I'd been sober for a year. I asked to visit. You wrote back telling me to stay away, that I had no right to see any of you again, not after my drinking had killed Charlie's parents."

"My God, Vi," Uncle Ed whispered. "It was the first letter he sent. You threw it away without reading it, but you wrote back to him. After that you returned his letters."

Aunt Viola was holding her chest, too stunned to speak.

Everyone looked shocked. But I was the only one who started crying. For all those years, Groover might have been in our lives—if only Aunt Viola had read his letter.

Groover spoke to Harry, his voice hoarse with emotion. "You told me to drive to Connecticut and try again in person. I was too ashamed. If only I'd listened . . ."

Harry made a dismissive gesture with his hand, as though waving Groover's mistakes—even Aunt Viola's—back to the past where they belonged.

My aunt's voice sounded weak. "Is this the truth, Charles? You haven't had a drink in six years?"

I tugged on Harry's sleeve to make him tell Aunt Viola that he knew it was the truth. His eyes were tender, but he shook his head. I guess he felt Groover needed to handle this on his own.

Groover whispered, "It's the truth, Vi, I swear. I'm so very sorry about everything. I wish I could live it all over, bring our sister back, give Charlie her parents, but I can't." His eyes were shiny with tears. "Give me this chance, Vi. Please. And give it to Charlie."

The silence made it hard to breathe.

Uncle Ed spoke up, surprising me. "We've been worried, Vi, that she has no friends living near us. We saw quite a few kids on the way here."

"I even have a best friend already," I said. "His name is Joey."

Aunt Viola still didn't answer.

Then Harry stepped into the silence. "This is still a good school district, Vi. I took the liberty of speaking to the principal. He said it's just a matter of transferring Charlotte's academic and medical records." He held out a slip of paper. "Here's his name and number. If you and Ed can stay over at the Inn, he's able to meet with you tomorrow morning."

"It's a beautiful inn," I cried.

She eyed the paper but didn't take it.

Her fingers caressed the carousel on the dresser, and the music box tinkled, then went silent. A guilt I'd never seen before came into her eyes, as she studied the toys in the room. She must have realized that Groover had sent me every one. And I guess they told her how much he'd always loved me.

When she looked at me, you would have thought she was watching the soaps. "Charlotte," she said softly, "are you sure you'd rather live with your Uncle Charles?"

Not wanting to hurt Aunt Viola's feelings, I hesitated. Finally, I said, "Well, I was looking at it this way,

Aunt Viola. You and Uncle Ed have each other. If I stay with Groover, it'll be even-steven."

Lifting her trembling chin, she cleared her throat. "Harold! Give me that paper with the principal's name on it before you use it for spitballs!" She snatched the paper from his hand. "We'll go to the school in the morning, Charlotte. I want to meet every one of the teachers." If she hadn't crossed her arms over her chest, I would have run right into them. "You can stay for the rest of the school year," she added. "I'm making no promises after that. If your grades drop—"

"They won't, Aunt Viola. I can get B's without opening a book!"

"Never mind *B's,* young lady!"

. . .

It wasn't until the following afternoon that I understood how big the change in my life was going to be. I'd only thought about staying with Groover. Not once had I thought about leaving Aunt Viola and Uncle Ed.

At the car door, Aunt Viola turned to Groover. "I expect to hear from you every week. . . . She doesn't like canned peas, only frozen. And she hates peas and carrots mixed. She loves macaroni with red sauce but not with cheddar cheese. I'll send you a meatloaf recipe; it's the only one she likes. And don't be letting her drink Dr. Pepper at bedtime. The caffeine gives her nightmares."

Uncle Ed caught my eye. He looked like he was waiting for me to understand something. I smiled at him because I'd understood right away. There are lots of ways a person can show love—even separating carrots and peas.

"I'll pack up your things and ship them, Charlotte. They should be here soon."

"No, Aunt Viola," I announced. "I don't want you sending anything."

Everyone looked surprised.

I took a deep breath. "I want to come to Connecticut and get my things—with Groover. I don't want anyone being mad at him anymore. And I don't want anyone feeling guilty about letters and presents and ferries. I want us to be a family!"

Aunt Viola folded her arms sternly.

I crossed mine just as hard.

She stuck out her chin. And I did the same.

We gave each other our best squinty-eyed glares . . . and I sure hoped I could outlast her.

"Hmpf!" she finally said, raising an eyebrow. Then she dropped her arms. "Charles, you bring her next week. You'll stay the weekend."

Aunt Viola turned away quickly before I could hug her.

Uncle Ed leaned down and kissed me good-bye. I whispered in his ear. "There's a Dumpster at the train station if you get any more roadkill."

His shoulders shook as he climbed into the car.

He started the engine but pressed a button on his side to lower my aunt's window.

"Charlotte," she said. "You call us anytime, day or night, collect if you have to."

"She won't need to call collect," Groover said. "I've got a good business here, Vi. She'll never want for anything."

He bent toward the open window, his arm around my shoulder. "You still have that old Volkswagen Bug, Eddie?"

"It's stored in the garage," he said.

"I'll give it a tune-up when we come."

"If the tires are bald, we know how to groov—" Groover's hand clamped over my mouth.

"Good-bye, Charlotte," Aunt Viola said, her eyes straight ahead. "Behave yourself. And mind your manners. You weren't raised in a barn."

"I will, Aunt Viola. Honest." Her window slid up between us.

The tears felt cold on my cheeks as I watched the car drive away. There was a hollow in my heart that I never knew Aunt Viola had filled.

Groover took his arm from my shoulder.

Suddenly I was racing down the street, my arms pumping, calling out her name. "Aunt Viola. Aunt Viola. Wait!"

The car screeched to a halt. Her window glided down.

I threw my arms around her neck and whispered in her ear. Her eyes grew wide, then she smiled. I figured Aunt Viola would want to know that Melissa got over her amnesia and realized she wasn't really Melissa, so she wasn't Dr. Tom's sister.

"Mother Superior made her leave the convent," I whispered. "She told her to give life and love another chance." Her cheek felt soft when I kissed it. And she didn't resist when I hugged her tightly.

Uncle Ed looked so cheerful that he popped the lighter in. The car wasn't halfway down the street when a puff of cigar smoke blew from the car. It made me smile when a second later the cigar flew out of Aunt Viola's window. I guess Uncle Ed had finally quit.

• • •

In the mornings, the sun filters through my curtains and I wake up in a pink glow. Robins have built a nest outside my bedroom window. In the warm sunlight, it sparkles with silver tinsel that may have blown all the way from Connecticut. With our eyes closed, Groover and I tossed flower seeds into our new garden so our life together would be filled with surprises. Every night before bedtime, he shoots hoops with Joey and me. Chuck goes crazy—he's our chocolate Labrador puppy— tripping Groover, slobbering on the basketball. Groover says we're in cahoots with Chuck, and he's thinking about getting another dog to help even the score.

But he still hasn't proposed to Roberta. Judge Harry

says Groover better learn how to handle me before he even *thinks* about taking on Roberta. She doesn't seem to mind. I guess she's been waiting for so long that she'll wait for as long as it takes. Sometimes she spots Groover watching her from the porch. She gives me a wink, then her walk gets jauntier, and her hips seem to sway ever so slightly. I know she's packing that kazoo. And I can't wait till we're playing ragtime.

Can I tell you a secret? At first I worried that Groover might drink some day, and I'd be plucked from his life like a rusty nail. But I don't worry anymore. If Groover can let go of yesterday, then I can let go of tomorrow. There's another reason I don't worry. Remember how I once thought I might have a guardian angel, washing up on the beach like I did, then coming back to life? Well, now that I found a home with Groover—where a rusty nail fits in like a silver peg— now I *know* I have a guardian angel. The way I figure it, she wants me living here because she shares my opinion of Groover. Honestly, I don't know what Aunt Viola was thinking: How could there be room for larceny in a heart so filled with love?